PRAISE FOR KAALCHAKRA

"The universe that manifests is a magical and vividly lush one populated with gruesome monsters hellbent on vengeance and peaceful warriors sent to protect and guide. The author differentiates the magical from the modern by using vivid descriptions of colorful and kinetic landscapes, gods, and monsters. Spiritual ideology is woven into powerfully rich dialogue meant to motivate and uplift. An immersive mythological yarn with a YA twist."

–Kirkus Reviews

"Spirited, swaggering fantasy...the action is fast, inventive, touched with poetry...there's much inventive vigor here, a deep engagement with demons both mythological and interior, and a rousing spiritualism. The characters burst with heart, and the storytelling is clear and exciting."

–Book Life by Publisher's Weekly

"Teen author harnesses power and wisdom of ancient myths."

–Outlook

"Teen author spins the Kaalchakra to connect with modern readers."

–Times of India

"Teen author connects Indian youth to their heritage. For a teenager to think of it is laudable enough, for one to do something about it is extraordinary."

–Mid-Day

KAALCHAKRA

THE RISE OF KALKI

AADITYA SENGUPTA DHAR

Anecdote
Publishing House
For the love of quality reading!

Anecdote Publishing House
2nd Floor 2/15 Lane no. 2 Ansari Road, Daryaganj-110002
Email: info@anecdotepublishinghouse.com
Website: anecdotepublishinghouse.com

Published by Anecdote Publishing House

First Edition 2024
2nd Reprint 2026
ISBN 978-81-963155-8-0
MRP ₹ 350

Book Promoted and Marketed by Champ Readers Pvt. Ltd.
Edited by Amy Brantley
Cover design by Aaditya Sengupta Dhar and Hubhawks
Layout by Graphic Tailor
Printed by Thomson Press (India) Ltd, New Delhi

CONTENTS

PROLOGUE

The thatched huts and thick foliage that covered the cliff were cloaked in a deathly silence in the night. The full moon cast its ghostly light, glimmering across the ocean, rippling with the waves to the foot of the precipice.

A *Pemangku*, a Balian priest, stood in pure white robes on the edge, overlooking the Indian Ocean. Ancient, hallowed phonetics flowed from his tongue, filling the quiet of the night around him with a sacred melody.

Vande Vishnum Bhavabhayaharam Sarvalokai-kanatham.

I salute you, Lord Vishnu, who removes the fear of worldly existence and who is the Lord of all worlds.

The priest stood, robes flowing in the frigid, gusting sea breeze, and gazed with raised head and eyes swelling with hope at the skies that shimmered with celestial light.

The Priest had just spread the heavy incense in the air and nourished the blazing flames of the shrine's altar. He dreamed in his soul, like billions of others, that the prayers of all devotees would collect in a storm that awakened the avatar of Kalki to give them deliverance. A deliverance into a new age of hope and peace, a turning of the Kaalchakra, the wheel of time.

But it was still the Kali Yuga. A time of death, depravity, and darkness.

There was a boom in the deeps, at the edge of consciousness. The priest's eyes widened as he heard a screeching noise nearby.

With the cold wind came a swarm of black forms, wheeling away inland, their shrill cries sounding the alarm for all other creatures around. The bats were fleeing. But fleeing what?

The sea tore away from its kiss with the land, waves pulling away, engulfed by the uncharted night.

Then they crept closer, foot by foot, until they gathered momentum and rushed in like black clouds, wreathing the shore once more, writhing, foaming, and roaring, seeking to destroy all in their path.

The priest quietened; his breath quickened; his eyes widened, as they gazed at the waves as they built up into a deluge; a torrent of water towering above the cliff and crashing onto it.

The thatched huts were torn asunder, fragments tossed far and wide. The thick bushes were cloven and ripped apart as if by monstrous hands. The priest saw moonlight through a gap in the crashing waves before he was swept under the tsunami, and then he saw no more.

***

On the walls, rimmed against a pitch-darkness, were small squares, the windows which gave the crew a glimpse of the terrible conditions outside. Through these, monstrous black waves rose and heaved. The captain looked through one of the windows, up at the open firmament of the skies, where the stars seemed to be mocking him, from far above the waves that were toying with his ship.

The captain clung on to the handles of his seat with one hand while commanding his crew to try and navigate their way through the stormy conditions. He was the captain of a US Navy survey ship that had been on station off the coast of Bali when the huge underwater tremor had been felt and the devastating tsunami unleashed.

He had the latest technology known to man at his disposal in this multi-million-dollar ship, but he, and all his technology, were mere playthings before the fury of nature they faced.

A voice spoke, quivering in the tumult, but uttering

words that rode the tsunami's tide and rang like thunder in the captain's troubled mind.

"Sir, our sensors are picking up radiation near the epicenter!"

"What? Where the hell would that come from? Who would…"

He never completed the thought, the unfinished question of who would have set off a nuclear explosion on the sea floor, when a gigantic wave crushed the ship, sending it to the bottom.

Somewhere far below, in the ocean, the explosion had been but a murmur in the bottomless deep of primordial malice.

It had been but a breath of wind, bearing the sweet smell of rotting corpses, chemical-infused waves, and fresh blood. A breath that whispered the dark desire for revenge, a desire that had lain dormant for millennia.

For Kali Asura had awakened.

ONE

Pull off in that Roadster SV, ah
Pockets overweight, gettin' hefty, ah
Coming for the king, that's a far cry, ah
I come alive in the fall time, I…

Hoodies swayed with the flow of the music, each syllable pulsating like a spark, rhythms and notes mixing in a verse that filled the washroom air.

Such was the immaculate vibe. For all save one.

All Abhay heard, gazing in from the door with glazed eyes and shoulders slumping with boredom, was a conjunction of electronic sounds and autotuned voices, played on an electronic device, from the music his friends were listening to.

He sighed, opened the door, took a deep breath, and strode into the school corridor.

He knew these halls well; the avenues of the school, in which students trekked in gregarious clusters, teachers stalked on patrol, and the paraphernalia of school hung on the walls: posters displaying students' work, printouts of the Learner Profiles, and silent, wooden doors with the three-digit room numbers gilded in gray on metal plates. His shadow glanced back at him from the blue floor.

But how well did they know him?

Anyone in the school would have said Abhay was smart, just because he got good grades and won several competitions. But any who got to know him or got a chance to interact with him regularly enough would say he was different. Sure, he was good at studies and liked reading and wore glasses. But his eyes would often glaze over during conversation with a deep wistfulness as if behind them, his mind wandered somewhere afar.

For while his friends whined about turning on the AC and were content with spending their lives roofed by the Mumbai urban sprawl and cornered in their narrow, insulated realities, his dreams were more often painted by starry skies and the screeching winds of celestial heights.

His hand closed around the handle, and turned it, as he walked into a large room with five rows of tables spread across it. The walls were bedecked with images of prominent historical figures- Hitler, Gandhi, Genghis Khan- and colorful maps of WWII Europe and modern India. Abhay walked to the front of the class and took his seat in the center, joining the steadily murmuring and shifting mix of students, settling into their seats.

From a desk to the right of the class, a slightly elderly woman arose, clothed in an orange sari, with a thick black mat of hair and eyes that twinkled as she spoke.

"Class, since we have one month left, why don't we do one quick unit of your choice? Any ideas?"

Three or four hands shot up straight into the air, including Abhay's.

"Yes, Abhay"

"I feel, Miss, throughout the year, we've been focused on modern history or Western history. I think we could look at ancient Indian history."

"You want to look at Indian history?" she asked, brow furrowing as she strained to think of something. Abhay could almost see those two words looming over her head, with the clashing of swords and the trekking of armies, and the laying of stone monuments that paid homage to ancient monarchs and even more ancient deities.

To her, it wasn't clear what would interest the kids amidst that confused jumble. But to Abhay, it was.

"Miss, why don't we learn about the Vedic Age? A lot of our culture, mythology, society, and history comes from there."

A groan grated through the class. There was something in that proposition that turned them off, though whether it was the image of Brahmans meticulously inscribing on documents or simple lethargy, or because it wouldn't be considered 'cool' to talk about 'old stuff', Abhay didn't know.

But as the words left his mouth, they seemed to trigger a certain response in the teacher. Her eyes sparkled; her head raised; her gait became straighter. *For,* thought Abhay, *though our words and fashion and lives may be Westernized, deep in our souls, we are all Indian.* He felt thus sometimes, his heart welling with joy and pride at the mere mention of myths and fables and legends, of the wondrous tales told and woven into the lifeblood of his country. At times, he wondered if they were tales at all.

But there was something else he saw at times. Because few others, certainly those of his age, seemed interested in that shared past. It was cool to know about the latest Western trends, but uncool to talk of our own past. Why was it cool to talk of reading Shakespeare, but uncool to read the Ramayana?

Like now, when the teacher took in the whole class. The glint in her eyes, the spark that had illuminated her disposition, was suddenly gone.

It was how the mere suggestion of exploring old tales and traditions seemed to deflate most teens. There was quiet in the class, as Abhay's words hung in the air.

Then the teacher straightened.

"Anyone else?"

The voice of a boy rang out confidently from the back:

"We could learn about the impact of nuclear weapons on modern international politics. That feels more modern and topical."

"Yes, let's do that," announced the teacher, authoritatively.

Abhay felt a spark set off in his brain somewhere, the embers of a fire burning within.

"But surely, Miss, learning about the past is as important as learning about the present? After all, that is where we come from, where much of what we see as 'Indian culture' was born. Especially these days, when very few of us understand our roots, covering this may be helpful and interesting."

***

Then it came, like the slithering of a snake through a forest, like the prick of a sharp pin- the high-pitched, mocking voice of a girl, that dripped conceit- well, that's how Abhay saw it.

The girl rolled her eyes at Abhay's typical *gyaan* and felt a pang of resentment arise in her. That over-smart nerd thought he was the only one in the class deserving of a voice, and always looked down on her, always keen to show off how much he knew. She'd show him.

She assumed her most generic assertive, academic voice, and spoke.

"Miss, I think learning about modern history is more relevant to our lives. Old stories will die out with time, but recent developments influence our lives and can never be forgotten."

She smiled triumphantly as she saw Abhay look at her, holding back an open glare, frustration festering on his face.

Who did the guy think he was?

***

Abhay turned, though he hated to, for he was met with that same smug grin, shining with vicious narcissism as the insouciant, relaxed eyes above it took in Abhay's obvious frustration.

The teacher paused, before clearing her throat to deliver her verdict.

"I agree with Ira. Let this be our next unit- the effect of nuclear weapons on modern global politics."

The next 40 minutes was a whirlwind of raised hands, fiery debates, and flashing slides and maps on the projector screen- in which both Abhay and Ira were curiously silent. They reserved a special disdain for the proceedings around them, and a simmering hatred for the other, never meeting each other's gaze, but throughout knowing what transpired in their minds.

On Abhay's black G-Shock watch, the 1 widened and curved into a 2, and the 9 vanished, replaced by a 0. It was 3:20, the end of the school day.

The students sped out like a rush of wind, gusting past, bustling and hustling, as they bolted for freedom.

Abhay found himself next to a familiar face- chubby and smiling as he strolled along easily with Abhay.

It was Vihaan, his closest friend in school.

But even as they began to move towards the stairwell, flanked by white walls and elevators, Abhay's ears picked something up, a derisive remark, cutting the edges of his hearing, as if goading him on to challenge its speaker.

"Unbearable, isn't he? Thinks he's some genius and we're good for nothing."

Abhay spun around and glared at her- a girl around his height, with flowing black hair. Her head was held high and eyebrows raised as if daring him to disagree with her. His breath stilled; his eyes narrowed. "What did you say?" he asked, in a low voice.

The girl leaned in, poking her head forward, eyes glaring through her flowing black hair that draped over her shoulders and face. She would not shrink back.

"I said what I wanted to, Abhay. I've never confronted you on what *you* say behind my back."

One of her friends pulled her back, but she shoved the hands off. As Abhay's friend took him away, she shook her head and marched off. As a teacher came in her path to ask her to tie her hair, she felt like kicking him and slamming him to the wall and was about to briskly stomp off, when her conscious, mature self caught up with her impulses, and she paused.

Getting out of control again, Ira. She closed her eyes for an instant, before opening them to the sight of a teacher, in his suit and tie, with his usual, artificially straightened posture, speaking in that same voice like a croaking toad…*Shut up, Ira.* She resumed a beatific smile and reached for her headband, struggling to wrench her lengthy black tresses into one ponytail.

Well, such was life. Be yourself, and everyone came out of hiding to pull you back in line.

Then she stopped. It looked like the teacher had paused and wanted to say something.

"Yes, sir?"

"Tomorrow, Ira, come to the Main Assembly Hall at 8:20."

"Why?"

Then she remembered, and she allowed her eyes to assume that sharp, questioning glance used by people daring those who don't like them to compliment them.

The teacher stared back at her, his eyes burning like the coals of a fire. She stared back. She won. He then withdrew a bit and averted his gaze. "You're getting an award- Sportsman of the Year."

"Sports…." She raised her eyebrows.

"Sorry- I mean sportswoman of the year."

She half-shrugged in exasperation. "Have a good day, sir."

She ran down the school staircases in a blitz and rocketed across the school astroturf, her ponytail coming undone and her hair billowing due to her speed. She opened the door of her car and slammed it shut, seating herself regally as her driver started the car. Tomorrow- the auditorium, with the whole school chanting her name. Today? Another soccer game in the park, before an evening with her father playing the guitar...and studies, when he insisted.

And no douchebag like Abhay to ruin it.

***

Abhay was meanwhile being ushered along, smoothly pushed away from the scene of confrontation by Vihaan. "Come on, come on," he soothed him, stroking his shoulders. "You know how she is."

"No, Vihaan. Yes, I know people talk about people behind each other's backs, but it seems like she has something against me."

"No, she doesn't. It's like what you say: put Kali and Kalki on the same planet, and one, or both, will be dead within 24 hours. Or something like that, right?"

Abhay stopped as they sauntered down the staircase, turned from blackish green to emerald by the sunlight streaming in. He seemed to gaze out through the window, an ashen stillness settling over his face.

"What's wrong?"

"What do you understand from that?" asked Abhay. "The Kali, Kalki, thing I'd said to you."

Vihaan grinned, with that disarming smile that made him so popular.

"To be honest, I have no clue. I said it so that you'd get your mind off Ira. What does it mean?"

Abhay thrust open the large brown door leading to the lobby, a well-lit room with trophies won by the school lined up in glass cupboards on the walls to the left, and a seating area of brown sofas before the reception to the right. He marched on towards the glass door, framed against the wall, beyond which was a lengthy path traversed by a throng of students and parents, leading up to the black and white school gates. His face seemed a flurry of thought and emotion as if he was trying to analyze his words himself.

"It means that two opposites cannot coexist. In this world, there is only room for one of either light and darkness, for one of good and evil. If the two spring up at the same instant, even for the length of one thought, one must go."

Vihaan was panting, struggling to keep up, both in movement and thought. Finally, the buses loomed up in front of them.

Abhay stopped. A neon-green parrot with a deep-red beak stood on the vehicle, trilling its birdsong, lifting its head, and beating its wings at the sun. Where the bird looked, clouds billowed past. One streamed by like the form of a celestial horse, complete with rapidly motioning legs and a rolling, swirling mane of hair.

Abhay grabbed the handle of the bus and wrenched the door open, leaving room for Vihaan to enter behind him.

Vihaan let out all the breath he'd been holding over that arduous trek in one sigh.

"Wow, that was deep."

Abhay shook his head.

"Why does this keep happening to me, Vihaan?"

His voice contracted to a whisper, and suddenly, it was small; small like a little child's, looking at the world with wide wondrous eyes and a tremulous heart.

"What does?" asked Vihaan, putting an arm around Abhay's shoulders. They were now on the soft, blue bus seats. While Vihaan reclined, resting his arms on the black arm-wrests, spreading his legs, and plugging an AirPod in to ready himself for a bus ride of vibing with his favorite rap tracks, Abhay was sitting straight, with fearful eyes that gazed at the trees planted at the school gate as if they'd fall over and crush the bus. It was a mark of Abhay's distress that he was sitting with Vihaan, and not at his usual place, and a mark of Vihaan's surprise that he didn't object to this unusual violation of his personal space and peace.

Abhay shook his head, dragging it through the thick, foreboding air. Everywhere he looked, there were signs. Omens. Symbols.

That was only when he was feeling mysterious, though, or "fey", as he liked to say: a word that meant surreally mysterious, as he'd learned from the dictionary. Even when he wanted to be normal and happy, there was always the vague impression of unease, of discomfort, of…a gathering. And not a gathering of storm clouds. Not the calm before the storm. Nothing that dramatic or poetic.

Random things- the stirrings of birds, the shapes of clouds, the perceived blowing of a horn on the breeze when he walked by the water, the adding up of disparate words from obscure places and dreams- words like "yuga", "deva", "asura - indeed, words like "Kali" and "Kalki". They seemed to fill the endless depths of his mind's ocean, while everything else was somewhere near the illusory, illuminated surface.

Again, as he got lost in these ponderings, he saw a golden discus in the sky, a blinding blur of motion in the darkness before it landed and turned into a large wheel of many spokes and intricate designs that spun into the night.

At last, he shook his head, as if seeking to break through this mental storm. It couldn't be real, could it?

Vihaan watched this with some alarm, and, with a voice, hesitant like a feather, slow like a polar bear plodding through thick snow, sought to lighten the atmosphere.

"Look, Abhay, here's some cool news I think you'd be interested in."

Abhay inclined his head to look at Vihaan's phone and saw there a news report, against the backdrop of a video of crashing waves breaking on a temple on a hillside.

"Tsunami wrecks ancient Bali temple and surrounding communities."

Abhay stared. In the black forms of the waves, in every curve, he felt his soul get lost as if they were claiming his heart too and filling it with a deathlike cold. Vihaan saw his expression.

"Arrey, I mean the one after this."

The news report abruptly stopped, and the screen swiped to the right as the Reel ended. Then there it was. A snow-covered mountain, a behemoth, solitary and looming up against the blue sky. Its slopes were curved like that of a pyramid molded with gentle bends and undulations as if from clay, or from the gathering of rock and soil over millions of years.

"'There have been new UFO sightings over Mount Kailash," announced an excessively grave voice. Then the camera panned, and changed to the view of a vast lake, with pure blue waters shimmering in the sun, the rolling forms of rocky, snowy hills and peaks in the background.

"Local people have reported strange lights and noises, especially at night, particularly around the two lakes- Mansarovar and Rakshastal, which in Hinduism represent the Sun and Moon respectively. These are far from the first accounts of strange sightings near the Mountain, where it is said, the god Shiva lives."

Abhay looked at the video and felt that same sense of wonder, of awe, of wanderlust, envelop him. It felt like the strange, thick cold that stuffed his mind for the past few minutes dissipated, and was filled instead with the invigorating, windy, freezing cold of the mountains, and he longed in his heart to journey there and see the mountain of Lord Shiva for himself, unravel its secrets and unearth the mysteries of the divine realm, of another world. Perhaps the UFOs, the lights, were but glimpses of a greater truth.

Then Vihaan broke the silence, and Abhay was there again, next to his friend on the school bus.

"Abhay, some of us planning a trip. We're going to Lonavala for three days over the long weekend next month."

Abhay returned his gaze, his eyes taking on some clarity for the first time in the ride. "I won't be going this time." And Vihaan knew he meant it.

"So…it's your grandfather?"

"Yes," said Abhay, in that grave, melodious voice Vihaan had noticed he reserved for those he loved. Which was, mostly, just one man. "My grandfather isn't feeling very well. He needs me to take care of him. He's the only family I have. And I'm his."

At last, the bus ascended a steep ramp, winding through several off-white, tall buildings before stopping at one. Abhay's home.

"Bye, Vihaan," said Abhay, tapping his friend on the shoulder as he got off the bus.

***

The bus's engine roared one last time and it rolled away along the rough pavement, out of sight, and Abhay walked into a warm embrace, into the comforting, familiar folds of a white, cotton shirt and pants, and the delicate build of a body that had known many years. From a height of six feet, a wrinkled face, lit by a warm smile, looked down at Abhay. Abhay held his hand, and the two ambled on, entering the vast, beige lobby, with intricate designs and marks of red-orange and black splashing the floors and walls.

"How was your day, champ?" asked his grandfather, putting his arm around Abhay's shoulders.

"It was great, Dadu," said Abhay happily. "What about yours?".

"Good," came the reply.

They took the elevator, and Abhay pressed "21". They exited the lift and entered the floor's common area- a short, plain, light-brown hallway, with a deep brown wall at the end, and two doors inlaid in it. Abhay's grandfather strode forth and unlocked the door, pulling it open, as Abhay entered his home.

It was quite spacious, with a large white sofa to the left once you entered, and a dining table further left. Behind the dining table was a kitchen, and further to the left a corridor began that branched into Abhay's and his grandfather's rooms.

They approached the sofa, and collapsed on it, reclining on the frame.

"Tell me about your day. How did the math test go?"

"It went well- the questions were quite easy."

"Did you revise?" his grandfather asked, leaning closer and listening intently.

"Yes, Dadu. Unlike last time there weren't too many questions, so there was more than enough time. I caught many mistakes I had made."

"Good!" was the reply. "I told you to revise! You're smart, but never get complacent." In such a manner, he went through the day, and, at many stages, his grandfather would ask him questions, eager to learn about some things. For a long time, they conversed, and neither of them tired of it, for they had grown close in years spent together, caring for each other, knowing that neither had any other family.

The evening passed by uneventfully. Abhay went about a typical evening of banging away on his keyboard to finish a school assignment, then getting lost in the folds of a book, before seating himself before the bright lights, booming music, and flying balls and fielders of the IPL Cricket match that was on TV.

Soon, night fell. The balcony, with its hanging chair and few potted plants resting on the white table, was wreathed in a twilight, blackish shadow, splotched by city lights, as was the full breadth of the windows that separated the house from it. Abhay and his grandfather sat in a warm interior made cozy by table lamps that illuminated the paintings on the walls- paintings Abhay had been told his mother had made. On one of them, the sparkling eyes and mischievous, curved smile of a three-year-old looked back, with a hint of a wink on his face.

Whenever Abhay looked into that portrait, it seemed as if his past, younger self was mocking him. Mocking him for knowing nothing of his parents- disappeared, presumably dead when he was four, leaving him in an orphanage where he was but one scared, worried, face among hundreds in sterile grey nursery halls. Then a retired army officer, with a deceased wife and no children, had picked him up, and given him a home. A man he now clung to as his grandfather, the only family in his life.

As night fell, they sat down for dinner. Paneer paratha was ready, and Abhay was glad for it, happy to not have the vegetables his grandfather insisted he eat more frequently. As he munched through the delicious food, a question sprang up in Abhay's mind. "Dadu, what is in that closet which you always keep locked? I have never seen the inside of it."

"It's nothing, Abhay. Just some old stuff. You would be disappointed if you opened that closet." They spoke no more of this, but Abhay secretly wondered why his grandfather guarded that closet so carefully and wondered if, in reality, something precious lay there. How he would love to get a peek inside! If only his grandfather forgot to lock it for a day!

The night outside darkened, until it was a deathly apparition, the black night sky tinged by strokes of deep ocean blue, with red and yellow indoor lighting from buildings adding to the tapestry. The small, white, gibbous moon, nearly full save for a region of shadow on its left, glanced down from the heavens, with a solitary companion star.

The time came for bed. Abhay's grandfather was already fast asleep on his wide, king-sized bed.

Abhay got up and walked onward, making for his room before he tripped on something on the floor and fell headfirst into a mass of polished wood. As his hand arose to massage the site of impact on his head, he paused.

For he gazed now into the dark, dim, depths of a closet packed with a swarm of medals and black-and-white and brownish-grey pictures of his grandfather and his comrades from the past. There were labels here and there, adorned with his grandfather's neat cursive hand, announcing years, wars, and places.

But at the heart of it all, at the base of the cupboard, under "1971 War", was a tablet. A rectangular, light-brown tablet, slightly larger than his palm, made of stone or hardened clay. On it were carved hundreds of symbols- symbols with little etchings and curving lines and sharp edges. In the darkness of the night, the edges of the symbols seemed to flicker with little gold splashes of light, casting an ethereal aura around each emblem. These were symbols unlike any Abhay had ever seen; symbols that seemed to emit some magic, some force, making the tablet feel heavy in his hands.

In Abhay's eyes, the world morphed for a split second into blackness, with only the tablet illuminating it, placed squarely at the center, the only source of light.

Shadows danced and fires flickered in the corners. The black crescent head of a long axe reared itself up against the ghostly-gray wall of the cupboard, casting moonbeams of white, pale light onto the tablet and Abhay's shivering hands, and came scything down in a terrifying arc…then it was gone, as Abhay processed, muted and indistinct, at the edge of his spellbound consciousness, the mutterings of his grandfather and the sound of metal clunking on his wooden bedside table, as he scrambled for and dropped his glasses. Hurriedly, Abhay shut the doors to the cupboard. The old man heaved a deep sigh of relief as he looked down at his grandson. "Ah, Abhay. Thank goodness it's you! I thought some *chor* had snuck in!" He guffawed but stopped when he saw Abhay's dazed face and wide eyes. "What happened?"

Abhay stood up and faced his grandfather. "I wanted to ask you something."

"What is it, Abhay?" asked his grandfather.

"I accidentally opened the closet you always keep locked. I tripped and bumped into it, and it was unlocked today. I…saw a tablet, inscribed with hundreds of symbols that looked like writing of the sort I've seen only in history books- like hieroglyphs from Mesopotamia or Harappa. When...What?" The last sentence hung in the air, unfinished, but Abhay's grandfather had understood what he was asking.

The old man smiled as he looked back through the decades, remembering the days when he was young and strong, waging war in the swamplands of the Kutch in Gujarat. His voice arose, "As you know, around fifty years ago, in the '71 War with Pakistan, I was called not *Dadu*, but Colonel Banerjee. This story is from that time. We were on patrol near the border with Pakistan in the Kutch. We had intelligence that Pakistan was coming across the Rann of Kutch. We wandered through vast woodlands, before sighting from beyond a hill a small complex of brick and stone. There was a solid perimeter erected from brick, and many rocks strewn about the place, with a few gently sloping ramps and raised platforms. This was the skeleton of a city. I was never much of an archaeologist and was rather bored by these dull ruins. We came under artillery fire, and we took cover in the ruins. When the firing ceased, I found myself covered in dust and cut in a dozen places from flying shards of rock. My men were only lightly wounded, and as we tended to our wounds and took stock, I saw that a large structure had suffered a direct hit and been blown to smithereens."

The old man's eyes were now animated, as he relived those days.

"It was then that I saw this tablet. It must have lain buried or concealed in that stone structure, but it was now lying in the open, amidst the ruins of that building. It was inscribed with hundreds of symbols in a script no one had learned to read- the Harappan script. I stared at it, wondering what it conveyed, what its significance had been in years that were all but forgotten by man. I don't know what took hold of me. I stuffed it into my bag and went on until I reached my fellow soldiers. Since then, I somehow have come to care for it, stowing it carefully away in an otherwise empty closet. One might say I keep it for memory's sake, but I have many better ways to remember those days, from photographs to my old uniforms, and have hardly ever stolen a glance at it for years. I…I just don't know how to explain it."

Abhay nodded and walked off to his room, the weary cloud of sleep slowly engulfing his mind. The world around him seemed to get dimmer by the moment, as he reached his room and groped for the blanket. The warm light of a bedside lamp seemed to revitalize his consciousness just before he switched it off, and, as if on cue, the doubts, the uncertainties that bubbled at the surface, exploded.

He thought he had known everything about his grandfather's past, so the matter of the tablet had been a rude awakening. The tale he'd just heard felt surreal, as if that tablet had been endowed with some guidance of providence that made it stand out from all the other carriers of Harappan script that littered the old sites of the Indus Valley Civilization.

In a moment, though, that wonder transformed into alarm as something sharp prodded his elbow, hard as stone. His hand sprang back as he recoiled, a shiver rushing down his spine. The tablet was back. In the shadow of the night its letters glowed brighter than ever, streaks of ochre and orange splashed across the darkness. Once again, the flurry of thoughts that usually rushed through his mind quietened to a whisper, a whisper that spoke only of the wonders and mysteries of the artifact. But, suddenly, even that was silent, until Abhay's mind was silent; unthinking, unfeeling. Only his hands moved, as if of their own accord- reaching for his phone.

At once, his fingers opened the camera app and clicked a photo of the tablet. Abhay wondered what had just happened and wanted to delete it, but his hands did not obey him, as they closed the camera app and went on Instagram. Abhay tried to stop his fingers, but it was of no use. The plus sign at the bottom of the screen was clicked, and the tablet's photo was chosen. His fingers then typed a caption across the screen, saying "A relic of the past in my grandfather's closet". And the picture and the caption were immediately posted, visible to whoever cared to check it. Abhay felt some strange foreboding as he looked at his latest post, but he did not know why. He had been a fan of fantasy and works by Tolkien lined his bookshelf, but the strange happenings of the last few minutes were more fantastic than any he had read in fiction. What was this strange tablet and why did he get the feeling that he was somehow being compelled to do things by forces beyond his control? He felt himself getting drowsy, and while part of him wanted to return the tablet to its rightful place, sleep overcame him in moments, and he passed out, into what he hoped would be a comfortable, dreamless, sleep.

But fate had other plans.

Long plunged into the drowsy, interminable caverns of deep sleep, Abhay's mind was silent; until it stirred, and his eyes saw light.

Only a misty, dim twilight, but a light nonetheless;

a reality, in more ways than he could imagine.

It seemed only too real when he stood three feet from his front door, in a hallway he knew only too well. It seemed only too real when he saw seven shadows; ever-changing, black clouds that stirred and shifted in a storm. Amidst the turbulence, there were glows of green eyes and the flashing of fangs, and his home's door found itself at the center of a cosmic hurricane of shadow and light.

Then from one shadow arose a mist of black tendrils, clenching and coalescing and swirling as they formed a fist, a core in which, for an instant, all the darkness festered.

Like a clap of celestial thunder, it crashed upon the door and smashed it asunder, leaving it a broken, bare frame of wood splinters.

Then there was silence.

Abhay awoke from his nightmare.

Only it had been no nightmare.

He now heard them.

Footsteps, great footsteps of a large company, prodding across the living room floor.

TWO

A deathly cry of terror arose sharply, shattering the silence of the night. Abhay froze. His grandfather!

He sprang to his feet, and hurtled towards the living room, shooting through passageways shrouded in blue-black shadow. His heart screamed in terror, and his terror screamed back; in the malevolent, hollow laughter from somewhere far ahead, in the flashes of pale blue on the walls, the black crescent axe silhouetted against them; in the flare of a flaming sword in the darkness. He soldiered on, his legs pumping, even as he stumbled in the pandemonium.

But he never got there. Just as he saw an explosion of light at the end of the tunnel, a force like a supernova smashed into his abdomen and sent him soaring through the air and nearly crashing into a tall mirror, before he stopped, in mid-air.

He could still feel, like rumbling thunder or quaking Earth, voices from the living room, but they dimmed to insignificant whispers and silence as invisible hands hefted him and hurled him headfirst into the window that erupted in a blast of glass shards ahead of him, though he felt no pain or suffered no bruises as if an invisible hand had shattered the window before him. Abhay looked down on the entire neighborhood of Hiranandani Gardens, Powai, a mosaic of buildings, streets, and trees, with the pale, moonlit, hill-nested Powai Lake in the distance.

He writhed and flailed his arms, but came down like a sinking deadweight through water, plummeting in free-fall.

He closed his eyes. He held his breath. He braced himself for impact.

It came, but only after he spun on his axis, his bare feet thumping into the pavement, his descent somehow slowed so that he came to no harm. He had made a perfect landing!

The night air seemed curiously weightless, as he bobbed up like an astronaut in deep space, free of the clutch of gravity.

Then Abhay's body surged forward as if sucked in by a black hole, and his body felt like it was cut in half as he raced forward like a shooting star. The world was a blur, light reflecting from the moon and the few stars in the Mumbai skies to splash across the heavens. There were hints of forest green, gray, blue, red, and white in it, mingling in a nebulous, ethereal cloud.

He felt like he had entered some parallel magical world with infinite possibilities and countless mysteries one could spend a thousand years exploring.

In this uncanny haze, Abhay saw a largely nebulous blackness rush towards him front-on. It came with a smooth hum of rubber against concrete, bearing brilliant lights on either side. But all of a sudden, Abhay felt himself being held as the same grip clutched him and effortlessly flung him to the side. The car hurtled on, and Abhay, somehow still on his feet, went on running.

But the jarring sensation of the force had jolted him out of his stupor, and his head buzzed with persistent thoughts. What was the force that pulled him away from his home, from his grandfather? Who were the people who had entered his home? Why was he being pursued? How had he survived the fall from the window?

These were followed by a powerful pang of shame-shame for forgetting the one family he had. He could only hope that his grandfather was alive, but tears fell down his face upon contemplating what may have happened to the man. These tears, these emotions, resonated with a fundamental part of his identity, and instantaneously their burden overpowered the ethereal, magical environment created around him. The psychological enchantment that'd been woven around him collapsed, torn to shreds, as Abhay was overcome by anger.

He filled his mind with wrath; he thrashed out violently; he convulsed in desperation. But none of it worked. He boiled with fury, cursing those behind all this, those who had plotted to kill his grandfather with their strange magic and deeds. But that rage was replaced by iron-hot pain in a second. When he resisted, it seemed like the force grew stronger and stronger, until the chains bore down into his skin and wrapped around every inch of his body. The pressure was too much for him to bear, as he cried out for help and begged for mercy. But the power that was controlling him seemed like lava from a volcano, charring his skin and dooming him to instant death. His shoulders slumped, his eyes shut, and he passed out.

Little did Abhay know that this affair was much bigger than he could fathom. It was much bigger than him or his grandfather, for he had gotten embroiled in the greatest war the world had seen in millennia.

***

Thunder rent the air. Raindrops gushed forth from the heavens, pelting down mercilessly upon the ground and splashing in the endless, black sea. Gray clouds gathered far above, filling the sky and casting dreary shadows amidst the dusky lamplit night streets and across the dark sands of Juhu Beach.

Ira was seated at the rain-splashed window of her

room. She breathed on it, leaving foggy watermarks on the glass.

She imagined being out there, in the eye of the storm. She imagined great tempests lifting cars and hurling them at her window, and blowing to smithereens the posh, placid buildings that lined the waterfront.

Would she be able to get away in time? Shouldn't be a problem for the number one athlete in the school, right?

Her reflection stared back at her, her hair an unkempt black mass draping over her shoulders and face after another night of rolling around, lost in incessant nightmares and troubled dreams. Her loose turquoise top, with "Magical" painted across it in silver, glowed in the falling rain, and she wanted more. She wanted more destruction, more natural fury, more thrill.

There was this restless part of her that longed to be free, like the dolphins that frolicked through the oceans of the world, like the birds that soared through the skies. There was also this primal, violent core in her that wished sometimes to be in the eye of a hurricane, riding the waves, or something beyond the mundane trappings of life.

Many people who scratched even the surface of her personality would be put off, perhaps terrified. It was a strange instinct, but she knew it to be true.

Shh, her mind said. *Getting out of control again, Ira.* And that was her sane side. She made a point of telling anyone she met that she was a logical, calm person; and staying awkwardly silent when her temper and passion threatened to make her do something that contradicted that.

But, in truth, she'd never understood logic. Sensibility. Prudence. Mathematics. Grades. They were all alien to her. "Understanding" was itself such a lame word. Immediately, she pictured standing under a bridge and looking at its foundations, its structure with comprehension. She preferred flying over the bridge-taking in the beautiful view of the river around it, and then soaring into the sky to revel in the world's delights. That's why she loved sports- breaking free of the mind's constraints, unleashing the competitive spirit and inner drive. That's why she loved playing the guitar, being able to lose herself in the rhythm and feed her rebellious spirit, feeling free of all the constraints and conventions that governed her mundane everyday life. *But,* she thought to herself as she gazed at the rain cascading across the sand and gushing from the sky, *your restlessness is the reason you can't memorize songs on the guitar or get some chords and inversions and that stuff right.*

Every day, she would play a bit with her father, who accepted her style of playing and helped her create melodies of her own.

Many kids she knew just loved their parents because they were parents- because of DNA. They didn't actually spend much time with their mother and father.

She'd never had a mother. Dead, apparently, along with her biological father. So, her dad didn't actually share any DNA with her. But that didn't matter. Her love for him stemmed from all he had done for her in raising her, yes; but that extra fuel for her love, that extra strength in the bond with him, came from how he loved her for who she was. No one else did, she knew. But that was okay, as long as he was there.

Then there was an eerie silence- a sudden emptiness in her erratically racing mind, spaced out as it pondered her life through the falling of the rain.

Then it happened.

That logical side would have said that the flood that now overwhelmed her was another nonsensical nightmare and fantasy. But she wasn't listening.

A voice boomed in her mind, slow and ringing with power and magic, pounding and reverberating like drums in caverns deep and ancient. Images flashed wildly in that tiny space, threatening to burst through its walls, breaking the dam and flowing out, lost forever in the firmament of the heavens.

"Ira," it said. *"I am Maya- your mother."* That word…that final word...she had heard it scarcely in her life. It seemed distant, even non-existent. Her father had been all she had. The thought had sometimes come, unbidden, wondering where her mother was, but her father had never answered her, only saying that he had adopted her when she had been very young.

Ira sat up straight. She had heard this voice before, in her dreams, and thought it to be nothing more than wild dreams born out of the regret of never having known her mother. But this was real. She was awake, and the voice was somehow speaking to her.

"Pay attention, my girl. You are in danger."

Ira's mind went wild as her shoulders slumped at the weight. In her mind, she saw a clay tablet, inscribed all over with strange, curving letters. Here and there amidst the forms, a bird flew, a fish swam, and a tree swayed in the breeze. They came together in lines of pictographs that spun around her and seemed to drag her into the depths of the dents formed by the deeply carved script. Then her brow furrowed as a boy walked in the darkness, staring fearfully at his surroundings. This...the glasses, the build, the walk, the fidgeting hands...this was Abhay! Part of her grinned evilly, seeing him scared and clad in a crumpled blue t-shirt and loose track pants, out in the cold, but another part of her hesitated. What did all of this mean?

The voice spoke again. *Ira, find Abhay. Find the tablet. Go with him. I will guide you, putri.*

Her fists clenched. She had just been called daughter. By her mother. For the first time in her life. In Sanskrit, it seemed, but so be it.

She was ready. For anything.

Then a thunderous roar resounded amidst the silence of the night. The door to Ira's room, bedecked with old pictures of her, running on a school sports day, smiling with her father, was smashed from its hinges.

In the doorway slumped the form of her father. His skin was deathly pale, and blood spurted from his mouth in bursts. A black hand seized his hair, fingers adorned with gold rings. It gripped a short, curved sword, placed at her father's already bloodied, slit throat.

"Daddy!"

In the stuffy night, a flame suddenly gushed forth and scorched the sword to ashes.

A blinding flash of light shattered the air, and like the thumping of falling trees, she heard bodies in the corridor outside hitting the ground.

The voice returned. *Run.*

But Daddy….

He's gone. For a few days. But I'll get him back for you.

And that was it. Part of her mind thrashed, roared in agony and loss at the death of her father. But amidst this cacophony of noise, of voices, of magic, she couldn't think of anything.

All that worked in her mind in that instant was a primal instinct that drove away all sense and emotion.

She didn't know what her mother was- demon, goddess, enchantress, fraud- but the only thing that mattered in that instant, when another bolt of flame shattered the window of her bedroom, was that she wasn't a hallucination.

Jump, putri. Go…

Ira leapt.

***

As Abhay came to, the air around him was cool. He started and sprang to his feet when his eyes were greeted with a dark green arboreal canopy.

The trunks of large trees were visible for as far as the eye could see. The wind howled in the night and leaves rustled. The sky was a pure, undiluted, bottomless black, untainted by the lights of the city. Abhay's eyes and heart got lost in the sky, freed to dream, by the light of the bright, nearly full moon, of the invisible stars and galaxies that were just beyond that coating of haze, so thin at this distance from the urban bustle.

For here he was- a kid, born and bred in Mumbai, lost in the wild.

Memories rushed back- shattered glass, bolting through Powai's streets, the force wrenching and throwing him, the agony, the loss of consciousness. The slightly befuddled fog of his mind seemed to clear, giving way to fear. These trees, this forest…this was the Sanjay Gandhi National Park. He had some snatches of memory from his school trip here a few years ago.

Those told him that more than the rustling leaves and thick, towering trees may be watching him.

For at night, when the sun and humans slept, leopards, the park's most elusive denizens, came out to reclaim their realm.

Abhay shivered in the freezing cold and ducked as the wind sent a branch falling through the air. He huddled under a tree, trying to come to grips with all that had happened. His eyes glazed over, and he saw the shadowy forms enter his house, his grandfather killed, and he himself clutched by some unfathomable power and taken far away, into this forest.

Who had made all this happen? What did they want with him? What was his fate? To die in the jaws of some beast in the wilderness?

Abhay winced as he imagined the scene- gore would drip from the predator's fangs, flowing like rivers of blood that make everything wither and die. Much like the blood that had suddenly appeared near the bottom of the tree, going pitter-patter, pitter-patter against the ground like raindrops against the pavement, pooling up at its base like a puddle that slowly grew in depth and volume.

He started suddenly, gasping in shock. Blood? Here? A great shiver went down his spine, and he wanted to be as far away from here as possible, out of the reach of this abominable beast that lurked in the shadows. For somehow, Abhay knew that the beast that came for him was far more deadly than any predator that lurked in this forest.

There was the sound of great feet sweeping away leaves and shrubs like a bulldozer.

And then it came, looming up above all else, its head higher than the tree from behind which it had emerged, casting an aura of fear and dread over the forest, blanketing all the life, suffocating it. Its terror pierced Abhay, striking him numb with fear. For no sound escaped his lips; no thoughts went through his mind; no smells floated up to his nose; and the wind and the leaves were silent.

It was an enormous shadow, almost twice Abhay's height. Where the eyes should have been were two great orbs, looking down upon Abhay amidst the night like two blood moons in the sky that had replaced the older white and pure moon, heralding the coming of a new world order with torment and suffering in place of tranquility.

As if in a halo of horror around its head was, erupting in all directions, a great mass of emerald green hair, glinting in the moonlight. Two sharp fangs protruded from the mouth, curving like scythes, and extending to the chin. Its nose was raised, like a wolf's snout. Below a chest crisscrossed with scars and gashes of dark-red blood, it was wrapped in a bright red loincloth. About its neck and on its wrists and fingers were draped a lustrous assortment of jewelry- rings, bangles, necklaces.

As Abhay took a closer look at the mane around the head, he could see that the creature to some extent resembled a lion, but it stood upright on two legs like a man. In its muscled hands, it gripped a great broadsword, which dripped blood, forming a pool where he stood. Trailing behind him was a dark red line that made Abhay gag, for never before had he seen this much blood, let alone the residue of dead victims slain by one of the ghastliest cosmic beings of malice.

Then, the eyes suddenly moved downwards until they were looking at Abhay's hand hungrily. It seemed that what were orbs a few seconds ago, had become real eyes, with eyeballs and some sense of purpose, as if they ravenously wanted something. Abhay wondered what the lion-man was looking at, but as he followed the eye's gaze, he realized that the beast was not interested in him- but the tablet.

For like orbs of fire, they sent their blazing radiance straight at Abhay's right hand, which still clutched the tablet.

He let out a terrible laugh, that boomed like the death of a star amidst the night, and advanced at Abhay, as he let out a guttural snarl. Abhay was a black belt in Karate and knew the discipline of the dojo, his knuckles grated by the hard stone floors as he did push-ups, his body hardened by the uncompromising combat of sparring. He had smashed wooden blocks with his fists and smashed his opponent's cheeks with his *mawashi-geri* kicks; but before this beast, all of that strength, that training, fell apart. The power of martial arts and personal resolve and fighting spirit was trumped by something far older and more core to human nature, from the days in which humanity hid in the dark interiors of caves in starless nights and heard the winds whistling and the wolves howling: fear of the predator.

Abhay ran, but in the heat of the moment his eyes seemed to go fuzzy, and his head spun, as he slammed into a tree trunk and crumpled to the ground. The beast was upon him, swinging his blade.

For the second time that night, Abhay braced himself for impact.

For the second time, it was rather less fatal than he'd expected.

An invisible force smashed into the monster's body, sending him sprawling backward through the air, his sword skyrocketing straight up into the atmosphere.

"Parashuram!", the monster roared, bellowing at the firmament in wrath.

Like the explosion of a supernova amidst the celestial depths, there was a sudden profusion of light in front of Abhay, sending beams of white light shooting everywhere like the rays of the sun, blinding Abhay momentarily, as he failed to bring up his hands in time. It seemed that the beams of light snatched up matter from the nearby air, and then gathered them all together at the light source, before exploding like a nuclear bomb, except one that brings no suffering, just happiness and relief, lifting the hearts of all who were fortunate enough to see it. It formed a spinning circle, which was suddenly filled with a background white as snow.

The lion-man was flung back, screaming out his frustration and terror, and disappeared.

An outline formed in the white, and out stepped the Chiranjeevi, the immortal warrior who was Abhay's father.

***

Her mother's hypnotizing voice, her urgent words shining through the darkness of her mind like stars, guided her along her winding road, through waste-infested, water-clogged alleys, lofty highways, and dense forests. These minor details were small stirrings on the edge of her consciousness; her mind was vacant, a bottomless, black vacuum, in which only the impulse to run existed. Ira ran faster than she ever had, faster than she imagined any human could run, as her mother's voice kept up a hypnotic chant in her ears.

Then she came upon a thick cluster of trees, shrouding a forest cloaked in a silent darkness. It seemed to her as if there was a straight path through it all, and she could see through the murk, in her mind's eye, a destination. Her resolved, concentrating eyes suddenly blinked and faltered as she tottered on the nebulous edge between indecision and blind faith.

Yes, said the voice.

And she was taken; taken by faith in the sacredness of the road ahead, by an unshakeable conviction that it was blessed by fate. Taken by the conviction that no matter what, she needed to do as her mother asked.

She plunged into the forest.

***

Out of the light came a swirling mass of saffron and orange and red and black, materializing in a man, at least nine feet tall. His towering legs were covered in golden-saffron robes, while there was a brilliant red-orange cloth robe across his upper body, draped over toned muscles and deep battle scars that glistened in the halo behind him. His mighty, tremendous forearms gripped the haft of a tall, golden battle axe around half his height, with a black crescent blade on the top. The blade of the mighty axe stood against the light like the moon in an eclipse, diffracting luminescence around it, rays that streamed towards Abhay and seeped into his heart, stirring it with wonder.

His eyes were still, and proud. He had a thick, black beard ringing his face, and his black hair was tied behind his head, its black depths ringed by a single, glowing crescent. He looked up at the moon and smiled, a kindly smile, almost incongruous for such a terrifying warrior.

Parashuram had seen many moons, many days and nights, and many ages, pass by as the *yugas*, the ages of the world, waxed and waned. His body, shaped into a hardy, battle-scarred being by years under skies raining with spears and arrows and *astras*, stood solid.

He moved slowly, but majestically, walking on the balls of his feet, with the grace of a dancer, or a warrior. He stopped close to Abhay, his robe billowing with vigor in the wind, as the rest of his figure and his axe remained motionless.

At last, he spoke, and his voice was grave and melodious, like the voice of someone whose breath was flavored by stardust or some cosmic power, ringing out amidst the night and quieting Abhay's tumultuous heart.

"Welcome, Putra."

Abhay stood with mouth agape; voiceless, motionless, and for an instant, shocked into thoughtlessness.

The man, at last, after an eternity of that slow, enigmatic expression, let out a smile. His stolid face sparking and coloring all over with warmth like the radiance of the Sun. Then he breathed, and in this breath was no otherworldly, high power, but the comfort of love; of love long denied, love that slowly bloomed in dreams dreamed at a great distance, in a solitary deep darkness.

"I am your father."

The next second, Abhay felt himself lost in an embrace, and he didn't find himself hugging an ethereal mass of magic, but a very corporeal mass of muscle and bone and cloth. Abhay saw in his eyes the hardness peeled back for a moment, parted by the gentle hands of love, as his round, wise eyes glowed and glistened with the joy of being a father. A tear spurted forth from them and shone silver, before flowing away smoothly, causing a leaf to rustle on the forest floor. The man's voice and throat, for all its former weight and the pulsing veins on the neck, choked. "I missed you, Son".

It seemed to Abhay that in his life till then he'd been a lone, withered tree in a barren, rocky desert, and now, he was an evergreen, young sapling in a forest, cozy beneath the boughs of a wide banyan tree that beckoned him into his arms.

After a moment of reunion, they came apart and looked at each other. Abhay beheld his father and exhaled deeply, letting out all the shock and ecstasy of the past few minutes. For within him, he felt like he was someone now; someone with an identity, with a past, with parents who had birthed him and had hopes for him; someone with somebody else to call home, somebody who cared for him and would save him when he needed it the most- something he needed sorely after the madness of the past few hours.

"Who…Who are you?" His voice was tinged with wonder and shone in the night air like a child's untainted happiness as he gazed at the stars with a loved one by his side.

"How are you my father?"

"I am Parashuram. I…." He paused and seemed to gaze at the heavens for advice, wondering how to sum up ages of existence in a few lines. Then he took in a deep breath, and spoke, his voice regaining its former gravity and texture. "I am one of the *Chiranjeevis*, the nine immortals who are to remain on Earth till the end of the *Kali Yuga*. I am the son of Jamadagni and Renuka. I have seen much in my life, but it was ordained by fate that I take penance in the Mahendra Mountain of Orissa and return only in the *Kali Yuga*. I returned here once, so that you could be born. That was fifteen years ago. Now, I have returned for an altogether different purpose."

He paused. A storm of questions and newly found answers, and the suspense of awaiting the profound tidings he was about to be told, raged around that pause.

"I have come here to be your guru. For it was foretold long ago by those above that the guru of the lord Kalki shall be Parashuram."

There was an implosion in Abhay's brain as every unresolved mystery about his mind, his life, his purpose- all those visions, his different way of thinking, his inclination towards mythology- was shattered, all disappearing and paling in significance before the cosmic revelation he'd just been granted. Now, curiously, as the moment arrived, all those images, fears, that mental noise, dissipated. Now, it was just him and his father, Parashuram, the sixth avatar of Lord Vishnu, together one night in the Sanjay Gandhi National Park in Mumbai, speaking of the fate of the world.

He was silent, trying to grapple with all he had just been told. But his father spoke.

"Take out the tablet."

Abhay, hand now stirring slowly, burdened with the knowledge that every moment carried unimaginable significance, reached into his pocket and produced the artifact.

Parashuram took it and held it close to his face. It seemed to Abhay as if the moon enlarged at that moment, gaining in brilliance and size before casting out moonbeams in one great thrust across the surface of the tablet as Parashuram lowered it and beckoned Abhay over to see them. The ridges of the pictographic forms now glowed white, as the ethereal light flowed through them, and the edges shimmered.

"Today is the 11th Waxing Moon- the *Ekadasi*- a day when all the energy of Lord Vishnu comes forth. An auspicious day, indeed. I met my son. You met your father. And now we will obtain knowledge that no mortal man has till date."

Then the bushes to Abhay's right were cloven apart as a hurtling mass of turquoise and black and brown smashed through them. There was a flash of eyes swelling and glinting in shock before the form of a girl fell right before them.

"Ouch," it said. Abhay glared at the prostrate figure with vexation. Who was she to interrupt his reunion with his father, his understanding of his place and fate?

Parashuram smiled, and Abhay noticed, with a certain incredulity, that his father's serene self straightened and smiled even wider at this new arrival.

Muttering uhmms and sorrys, the figure raised itself up, found itself facing the battle-scarred form of the immortal warrior, and shrank back, nearly slamming into Abhay, who stepped aside. Then she paused and stared at him. Her jaw dropped, her eyes threatened to bulge out of her sockets before her skin started coloring with a sudden welling of glee at having found the object of the quest her mother had set her on. "Why are you here?" she asked, her face glowing with excitement as she struggled to keep her voice level.

Abhay stared too, but more in disbelief and annoyance. Ira? Here? What business did she have with the gods? Then she frowned at him; her smile disappeared, eyes quietened, and she was the usual Ira again.

"What do you mean, what business do I have? Oh..."

She raised her hand to her mouth, but then her eyes gleamed again and her mouth opened in a scarcely believing smile. Abhay hadn't really *said* that, had he? Inside, the voice of Maya spoke. *Yes, my dear. Sometimes, you can read minds.* "Really?" *Yes.* Then her mother sighed. *Looks like I'm going to start your lessons in illusion soon. You can't be so easy to read all the time.*

The voice echoed through her head, and life for

Ira was brilliant. Her mother had arrived, and she was on the cusp of receiving lessons from the greatest enchantress ever. Come to think of it, amidst all the running and death, her mother hadn't told her yet who she was.

And her father was dead.

Her gaze fell. She felt a lump in her throat, a pain in her chest, and her sudden thrill and euphoria crashed, lost in stormy skies of loss and upheaval. Tears flowed forth thickly, running across her face and mingling with her hair.

She took a deep breath, but her breath was hollow, a mere rasp in the stale air. "Daddy..." she croaked before her eyes closed; her face and skin lost color; she swayed and crashed headfirst onto the forest floor.

THREE

When her eyes opened, her vision was blurred, shrouded in tears, and all she discerned was a nebulous, fuzzy mass of gold and green. The night had been terrible. The worst of her life, by far, and the worst she imagined she could ever have.

The moment of her father's death had played itself out in her mind numerous times, scoring scars all across her traumatized mind. Her head throbbed with agony, and the golden light brought heat that seemed to scorch the surface of her scarred brain. Jerkily and with great effort, she wrenched her right hand up to wipe away her tears.

It was dawn in the forest. The trees were glowing neon-green, and the sun shone bright overhead. Spotted deer flitted between the trees, and a few birds chirped their song, their cheerfulness seemingly mocking the agony Ira felt.

She let out a long, bereaved, sigh. Amidst all this light and life, she felt withered and alone and could feel her heart, her will to live, dying bit by bit in her. It felt like her soul was decaying every minute, with little cracks running across its surface.

She got up, pushing through the thick air in front of her, and sat up. She continued gazing at the sky, wondering what she had done to deserve such an evil twist of fate that night- to discover her mother, and to lose her father.

She lowered her head and buried it into her hands once more, taking shelter in the one thing that remained untouched- the darkness.

***

Abhay and Parashuram sat on a large rock, overlooking the sunrise in the distance. The horizon was splashed with deep orange and the vivid colors of the sun as it rose in the sky.

Abhay's body was frail, bereft of all its strength and life, as he lay like a dead tree, felled by misfortune and loss. In every ray of sun in the sky was the sparkling smile of his grandfather. In the rustling footsteps were his footsteps as he took his weekend morning walk with Abhay. In every wind's whisper was his gentle, loving voice, as it cradled Abhay's heart in every syllable, accompanied by tender strokes of his hair, hugs, and kisses.

Now, Abhay, with his tear-splattered face, the coating glistening in the dawn sun, was resting on the chest of Parashuram. He was enveloped in his father's arms, taking shelter in the new family he'd discovered.

All night, Abhay had convulsed in writhing agony at the ghastly visions he saw, nightmares that taunted him- the son of Parashuram, even the supposed "Kalki", who had failed to save his grandfather, and had so callously gone along with the new developments, such as the coming of his father, without properly mourning the man who had raised him all these years.

He had struck out, lashing out with arms and feet at the phantoms that relentlessly haunted him; he had screamed, screeching in sheer terror at the sudden coldness in his heart, at the sudden void he felt open up within and threaten to consume him completely.

All through that, Parashuram's grip had not slackened; he'd held on, now and then chanting a *mantra* to bring peace to Abhay's mind; or merely muttering soothing words from a father to his son to chase away the dark.

Even his treasured *Parashu* axe, which he'd almost constantly held for millennia, lay now at his side, balanced on the small crevice between two rocks. Parashuram had space and time only for his son.

Abhay had asked him, in the past half hour, breaking the silence.

"What did the tablet say?"

"The girl must be present when that is revealed," had come the reply, and Abhay had not the energy nor mental space to devote an ounce of further thought to the matter.

They gazed upon the orb of the sun. As it rose further and further, progressing from deep orange to a brighter shade, it wreathed the panorama of forest stretching out before their feet in a golden mist. Then Parashuram spoke.

"We can resurrect your grandfather."

Abhay's head, swaying gently in the wind, stilled. His glazed eyes colored with hope, and he turned to look at his father.

"I vow to you that, in seven days, you will see your grandfather again in the world of the living. You will touch him and feel the warmth of life, hear his tender voice, and find peace in your disquieted soul. But that all depends on you, and what you choose to do in the next seven days."

Then there was a silence. Abhay pondered this, his eyes now fully alert, mind racing, like an explorer surveying the stars to chart his voyage. A flurry of emotions frothed and buzzed, but he quieted them. There was something in that pause of Parashuram's, something expectant, like his grandfather's when he would wait for him to repeat important instructions, so that he may remember them.

"What must I do?"

Parashuram got up suddenly, his majestic form and sable axe blade radiant in the morning light. Abhay sat straight and beheld his father before him, a living manifestation of Lord Vishnu himself, and he knew in his heart that the words that would be spoken then would carry weight for the very fate of the world.

Parashuram's eyes blazed with celestial fire; his hands gripped his axe hard, with the devotion of a true warrior, and his limbs and chest were infused with vigor. He paced about the rocky hillside, framed against the morning sky, every stir in his form imbued with purpose. He spoke, and his voice boomed in the air like the conch of the Lord Preserver of the Trinity that ruled the Universe, pronouncing prophecies of creation and destruction, life and death.

"You and Ira must embark on a quest. A quest to reach the gateway between Heaven and Earth on Mount Kailash in the Himalayas and restore this tablet"- he held it aloft, and all its letters and pictographic forms shimmered in sunlight- "to its rightful owners- the gods. For a great evil pursues this object- the Kali Asura, the demonic scourge that would reduce the world to a hellscape of wrath, and bring apocalypse in the *Kali Yuga*, the age of darkness."

Behind, staring at Parashuram from in between the bushes, was the bedraggled figure of Ira. The wind parted her disheveled hair, which streamed in all directions. From her ashen face, her moist eyes gazed expressionlessly upon the towering figure in front of her. Parashuram beckoned to her to join them, and she walked towards them, slowly and uncertainly, before settling on the ground next to Abhay.

"Abhay, if you triumph in this quest, your grandfather will be resurrected. Ira, your father will be resurrected. They shall return from *Patala*, the Realm of the Underworld, and live with you again. This boon shall be granted to the saviors of the world, to the last scions of Heaven in the mortal world, the fated restorers of light and justice in the corruption of the Kali Yuga."

At these words, the shadow passed from Ira's face; her eyes shone once again with hope, burning within like the fires of the stars, blazing like the morning sun. Her lips creased out gently in a smile, as if soothed by loving hands, and tears gushed from her eyes; but these tears were clear and smooth, like rivers of joy streaming down her face.

Abhay felt the shadow of loss pass from his heart, and the curtains parted on a new dawn.

But there was something else; his heart, so free, liberated for a moment, suddenly lay still, as if in expectance, waiting uncertainly on the cusp of... something. He met his father's gaze, as the sixth avatar of Vishnu finally looked up from the tablet to meet his son's eyes.

Abhay's mind caught up with his heart, and it seemed evident to him, as he looked at the tablet, what he needed to know. His determined, settled eyes turned up to his father's face.

"What does the tablet say?"

Parashuram glanced at Abhay and Ira, as if to ascertain their readiness, before at last looking down at the tablet.

"*Wrecked grhas, on rocky shores,*
Blasted asunder by the bolt of lore,
A crooked smile on the ocean floor,

From his slumber shall awake,
A scion of Vishvam incarnate,
Chiranjeevi's son shall rage,

But his is not a solitary fate,
Illusion shall with destruction create,
A girl to war for light in the darkest age,

With the wings of wisdom, the pure white mane,
With Nataraja's axe and Maya's mage,
And lightning in arms, legs, and tail,

Sorrow and Decay, Wrath and Plague,
Fear and Hell, and waters that rage,
All these the two heroes must brave,

By the twin celestial lakes, in seven days,

Through Heaven's mountainous gate,
They shall battle for the world's fate,

This prophecy of the darkest age,
Must be transported to on high, safe,
Then only will the first lingam be saved.

The Kaalchakra heralds a new age,
Bathed in peace, or wrecked by rage,
Determined by the struggle Kalki must wage."

There was silence. The words of Parashuram seemed to slowly settle in the next few moments, turning from mere words to an irrefutable truth. The trees, the rocks, the wind, the hills, soaked up and assimilated them into the fabric of their existence; for the prophecy governed all their fates. Even time and the very space around Abhay and Ira seemed to curve and undulate, as if wrapping around this new destiny.

Abhay and Ira had stood still for the entire poem, looking into the air with a kind of expectant focus achieved by those who are on the path to enlightenment, to acquaintance with a higher truth that would change their lives forever. Now they both relaxed a bit, their shoulders sagging, breath exhaled, as their minds had been freed of great doubt.

Ira spoke at last. "I understood the parts about us; I understood what we must do on Mount Kailash.

But the rest…they're riddles; and although I feel as if I am on the edge of solving them, as if their meanings are pre-programmed somewhere in my head, I…can't quite explain them."

She looked up at Parashuram again, her face angled upwards, facing the streaming sunlight, awaiting more answers.

"We are in the five-thousand-one-hundred-and-twenty-fourth year of the *Kali Yuga*. In this age, it has long been prophesied that the Kali Asura, who seeks dominion over the world and to plunge it into a hellscape of darkness, shall war with Kalki, the tenth avatar of the Lord Vishnu. The *Kali Yuga* is the most ghastly of all *Yugas* to befall this world; many terrible things are prophesied to take place, but they are each of them mere individual melodies of discord, strife, and depravity that collect to orchestrate the downfall of humankind and of the present Universe. The very existence of the Universe, even the predominance of the order of the Devas that has fashioned and ruled all Creation, is imperiled by Kali Asura and his children and Asura allies. Kalki is the sole champion of the world in this dire hour."

He paused, looking at Ira and Abhay, both of whom were hanging onto his every word.

"The prophecy foretells that the *grhas* shall be destroyed. Grha is a house; and temples are built as homes of the gods. This has already begun to manifest. This weekend, a temple in Bali was destroyed by a tsunami. A few days before, the temple complex of Angkor Wat in Cambodia was similarly desecrated and laid to waste. Next shall follow the core sacred sites dedicated to the Trinity- to the Lords Brahma, Vishnu, and Shiva, beginning with the Somnath Mandir in Gujarat. In the Somnath is placed the first Shiva lingam, which the tablet tells us will be destroyed if you two fail.

The destruction of these sites, besides being the most heinous sin committed in all history, shall be fatal for humankind, and the Earth. For the Lord Shiva has revealed, in ages past, that the sacred temples are the final reservoirs of divine blessing and power on this Earth, sending out celestial energy that shields the world from imminent catastrophe. Kali Asura and his forces seek to wreck these holy sites and thus strip the world of its protection; then the evils of the Kali Yuga shall be greatly worsened, and out of proportion from what has been ordained by fate, ruining the balance in the Universe, turning the Kaalchakra, the wheel of time, in a new direction. They have already begun."

He held up the tablet to the sky.

"But this tablet? If they gain possession of it, the world shall plunge into the void of cataclysm in a far more wicked way and cease to be the home that you know. That is why," he said, now pointing at Abhay, "after you posted the tablet's picture on the internet, one of the sons of Kali Asura came hunting; not you, but the relic. You are indeed a 'scion of Vishvam incarnate'- my son, and I am indeed an incarnation, a manifestation of the Lord Vishnu in the mortal world. As for Ira, you are indeed the daughter of illusion and destruction- of the Asuras Maya and Pralaya, whose names carry those meanings.

There is much else; but this is the heart of the matter; the purpose that you must relentlessly strive towards, through crashing waves and raining hellfire and swinging blades seeking to drown you in a sea of blood. I shall be your teacher, guide, and protector; for it was pre-ordained that I will be the guru of Kalki."

Abhay and Ira took in all that had just been said, these tidings, these pronouncements of their roles as champions against the darkness, against the horrific hordes of hell, against creatures whose malice and might their minds, so used to the comforts and trappings of modern life, couldn't even comprehend. But speaking of being champions...

"So, which of us is Kalki?"

Abhay looked dead straight into his father's eyes and asked the question that had been burning in Abhay and Ira's minds ever since Parashuram began his doomsaying.

Parashuram's eyes seemed to tense as if battling great cosmic forces that raged somewhere in their impenetrable, impassive depths. He glanced rapidly at both Abhay and Ira, and it seemed as if his gaze flashed…fear.

At last, he spoke.

"Both," he whispered. Ira nearly heard, on high, a thunderbolt renting the air and tearing asunder the ethereal atmosphere that Parashuram's words had created.

Abhay's lips moved, at last, as if stirred by that clap of thunder on high. Abhay's eyes turned red for a moment, his facial muscles tensing, his breath quickening, his poise straightening, his legs bracing for running. A storm suddenly raged in his mind, as if stirred up by that single word- tempests thrashed, storm waves surged and roared, and primal rage growled in his heart.

He closed his eyes, straining to break free of this heightened sense of terror and alertness. His pulse quickened, before he looked into his father's and then, strangely, Ira's eyes. She shrunk back from his gaze, feeling a fear she had never felt around Abhay, for all their mutual animosity in school.

Looking at her brought quiet to his soul, and at last, there was no storm- only an emptiness, only a warm cushioning his lungs sank into as his breath left him like a fuzzy cloud of warmth.

Breath hollow now, he looked up at his father again; but his voice was hoarse, almost rasping, thought Ira, as she trembled at this brief but vicious display of wrath from Abhay.

"She is an Asura. Isn't she one of *them?*"

"Such is fate," said Parashuram simply. His voice was light as if speaking of simple matters of no consequence. He smiled at Abhay and Ira.

"Much has been destroyed in our cosmos due to the ancient war between the Devas and Asuras. Perhaps it is only fitting that when the young of both lines can put that behind them and unite, that the age of discord will end."

In an instant, Abhay's mind was cured of its anger, and as if through clear waters he saw the truth, lucid and perfect, for it was ordained by the Devas themselves, and delivered by his father. Suddenly, his eyes cleared of their fey mist; his mouth was agape, as if in the shock of sudden clarity, before shutting, lips settling into a firm look. He paused and bowed his head in shame.

A hand lifted it up, and Abhay looked into the eyes of his father. Their sable black depths gazed at his face, Abhay found strength within them and nodded his head once.

"Abhay, the world is not as simple as divided into good and evil. For who are the Asuras, but the estranged kin of the Devas? We were together once, and you have the opportunity of bringing that balance back again."

That was the end of it. But Ira, standing a few feet away, pondered the scene, and even as Parashuram bade that they move on, saying "The Himalayas are a long way away" or something like that while he held the tablet, the strange scene stuck in her head and troubled her.

***

They walked onward. The morning sun rose higher until it was directly above them, illuminating the wide wheatfields they walked through, ringed by dark green rolling hills, with acreage of smoothened out light-green pasture stretching into the distance. The lush green forests they trekked through, leaves rustling underneath their feet, and joined the rolling, flowing streams and waterfalls in a calming ambient whisper. In this tranquility, it returned; the airy, ethereal voice of her mother, speaking in Ira's mind like the voice of an angel from above. But Ira's mind was not peaceful; it was raging with questions, with doubt, with fear. Her mother had been speaking to her for the past half hour, soothing her for the loss of her father and motivating her, assuring her of the powers she had inherited and that they could save the world and resurrect her foster father. Ira had heard these words, but, contrary to her mother's hopes, they didn't inspire her and invigorate her with newfound strength to complete the quest and find her destiny; they were, at some level, merely noises, a faint, faraway racket that strained to reach the midst of her stormy mind. For Parashuram's words, the prophecy, and Abhay's reaction, had somewhat dimmed the initial euphoria at being the daughter of a supernatural being and made her question who that supernatural being really was; indeed, who *she* really was. Part of her mind berated her, saying that faith in the prophecy and her mother was essential. Was that the logical part of her mind? She didn't really know anymore. The line between the rational and the impulsive Ira was blurring, fading in all the magic and revelations and doomsaying. *Shut up*, she told herself.

Focus.

Anyone with a father named "Destruction" and belonging to a race usually thought to be the cosmic bad guys deserves to question things a bit. Abhay had been right, hadn't he? Wasn't she an Asura? A demon?

There was a pause. A pause in her mother's monologue, a rupture in her unperturbed sense of calm. Ira felt some of that returning; that wildness she'd so often felt before, like the time she'd been gazing at the storm from her building minutes before being whisked away from her house. To question was her birthright, but so should getting some answers be. No matter if her mother was a master of illusion and telepathy.

Ma, Parashuram and Abhay said I'm an Asura. Am I one?

A long, drawn-out space; a space in the ceaseless flow of thought and conversation her mother seemed to revel in. Then, at last, her mother spoke, and this time, Ira felt the real weight of her force; the magic wasn't just in smoke and mirrors, and the illusion wasn't just tricks of mind play- they were true celestial forces.

Yes, you are.

But Ira didn't feel the panic she'd expected; none of

the breathlessness, none of the snatches of nightmares of red eyes and knives and bloodlust she'd thought would come with her unmasking as a member of that race. She leaned on a large slab of rock beside a small waterfall, taking a rest on something physical and tangible, lest she get lost in the unreal maze of her thoughts. Parashuram saw her stop, and somewhere on the edge of her vision, her eyes picked up him wrapping an arm around Abhay's shoulder and guiding him behind the nearby grove of trees.

But Asura means demon…?

It began as an assertion, one of those despairing assertions made by the lost, reaching for some clarity, some fact that remained unquestionable in the confusion; but it ended more as a question, as if Ira was clearing out even more space in the emptiness, for her mother to come and fill with the truth.

The word Asura has many meanings- the Mighty, the Powerful, the Celestial. The Creator made us long ago as fellow celestial beings with the Devas. We all have our own powers that distinguish us as primordial beings with a purpose in the cosmos.

Ira's eyes widened as these truths were breathed into her mind; for it didn't seem to her as if her mother, sitting in some distant heaven, was saying these words- merely that her all-seeing, all-powerful, celestial consciousness was passing on this sacred knowledge to her daughter's frail mind. Ira felt like she'd but taken a step into a bottomless ocean of secrets, the uncharted depths of another world of mystery in which she would discover much about her roots, about where she truly came from.

She took the plunge.

Tell me more about you, Ma.

The deity Brahma, whose each thought waxes and wanes like a celestial moon over millions of worlds, and who fashioned this Universe, had a son. A son who revolted; a son whose wild, raging mind liked less the quiet, serene heavens and more the untamed, wrathful worlds outside the Deva's supervision; where galaxies collided, stars exploded, where vast plains lay ungoverned. He was branded with the name of Adharma- "that which is discordant with Dharma (the righteous path)- and sure, he did commit a number of sins, wrongdoings; for his feral soul knew no bounds, only an insatiable lust for spectacle, for devastation and glory.

His children were thus, in the eyes of all, cast under a shadow of malice and sin.

He had many children, and they had children, who were my parents. I was called Maya, meaning "illusion", for my calling was the mystic arts, and at a young age, I attained mastery of conjuring. Kali, meaning suffering, was my brother.

"And I'm your daughter," said Ira; this time aloud, for she found that her heart, after learning all of this, no longer wished to keep her parentage, her identity, her being secret, like some clandestine, shameful, truth.

There was a nod somewhere; or maybe a mere affirmation, a silent signal from mother to daughter, which didn't even need to be made- it had always been there, a bond made in the very molecules of DNA that made up Ira, in the heights of Heaven or some other world where Maya had met Ira's true, biological father, and had a child with him.

But then, as the daughter of two Asuras, how am I part human?

You are not, my Putri. You are full Asura; for our true essences, our true beings, inhabit not the physical plane, but the vital plane- a region of existence above touch and appearance and even thought, where mortals go not. We are immortal. So are you. Though you have taken up this manifestation of a human to fulfill your crucial cosmic purpose, you are as eternal as I.

Immortality. As a child, Ira had thought it was little more than another excuse for the games humans and gods played; humans daring to search for the elixirs to eternal life, only for the gods to punish them. Now, her mother, this Asura, one of the most powerful beings in the Universe, was telling her that she, a 15-year-old girl from Mumbai, had this trait.

Her mind was silent; there was nothing to say, nothing to get restless about or overthink. At last, it reached for words; for ways to frame those neurons and pent-up shock into little sensory sentences. *Who has ever had an experience like this? Who had the whole story of their existence, their identity, transformed in just one day; their lives infused with such new vitality and force, their horizons stretched till the edges of the Universe?*

But still, there was a part of her mind that moved like a young girl, trying to make things a little more relatable with little comparisons and analogies. She pictured a whale in the deepest part of the deepest ocean, all alone with her slowly revolving dreams and brewing desires and thoughts, thousands of miles away from other life. She laughed aloud at herself, comparing an otherworldly, divine, life-changing experience with something anyone could see on National Geographic. But there was something else; for one moment, she cleared her head of this wonder, to pose one question to her mother; something that still nagged her, like a small floating pebble bothering the whale.

Why didn't you tell me any of this before I asked you?

I thought there was some fear in you. Some part of you that would wish my words away, that would flee from your true being and calling and the rare power your ancestry bestows upon you. I had no choice when Kali decided to unleash his plan.

Ira looked up. Sprawling over the space before her was a banyan tree, with thick foliage growing off a winding network of long, twisting, hanging branches. She thought of the roots of the tree, extending deep into the underground, roots that nourished the tree by absorbing water, assimilating minerals, that would form the organism's lifeblood. They gave it a sense of identity, of life.

She'd scoffed at Abhay when, with what felt like false or at best, misguided passion, the boy had ranted, on numerous occasions in history class, about roots and past identities and mythologies. But she understood it now.

Without this knowledge, she'd been like a withered, dead log of wood, bereft of nourishment and connection to a source of power. Now, she was secured to the soil, and from that celestial reservoir was drawing motherly love, heritage, and the powers of the heavens. She was, slowly, growing into a tree in her own right, sending her long, intertwining branches across the landscape and evolving into a being of potential and power beyond imagination.

There were no words to explain thoughts like this, and it seemed like her mother knew that, as a soft layer of quiet and comfort spread and settled across her mind, cloaking her mind in a world of peace and love.

I love you, Maa.

I love you too, Ira.

She shook off the crutch of the rock and stood straight, alone in the forested landscape. Water gushed behind her, birds chirped before her, trees swayed in the billowing wind; and in everything, in every breath, in every ray of light, in every stir of life, was the presence of Maya. She could feel it. At last, the void that had opened up to consume her upon the death of her foster father, the winds of bewilderment that had kicked up when she'd been thrown into a world beyond her understanding, all cleared. Her chest was free now, unburdened, and her mind was truly lucid. She felt like a bird, like an angel, like a god...like an Asura.

The sky was the limit. Or was it? She could see, in that moment, with her mind's eye whirring like Vishnu's chakra, pulsating stars and their planets spinning by, and her soul transported to paths never traversed by mortals. There was still more to learn, she felt, still more depths to explore in this uncharted ocean, still more unanswered questions. But that was fine with her.

She was at last in a world where restraint and logic had no place. She was at last somewhere where all the power, all the restlessness that had been but an inconvenience in her mundane, mortal life, could be set free to create spells and works of magic to destroy the forces of darkness and reunite with her father, and bring in the breaking rays of dawn on a new world. She had much to learn, but she had the best possible teacher- the mistress of illusion, her mother.

FOUR

The hours lengthened. The three of them continued their journey through forest and grassland. Living in Mumbai, and with his grandfather, Abhay had never traveled much, let alone trekking by foot through the wilderness.

At first, it had been thrilling to hear the birds chirping and see the deer flitting by. He'd felt a particular childlike joy well up in his heart when the chatter and cries of monkeys filled the air, and a mother Hanuman Langur, with fine light-grey fur and a charred face, appeared. He recalled a legend he'd heard about once, in which Hanuman Langurs traced their black faces back to the Lord Hanuman himself. When the monkey god had nearly been burned by the fires of Lanka, these beings had saved him. Thus, their faces were burned, but thus also were they blessed for posterity.

The Langurs had always been Abhay's favorite animals, for he'd loved the idea of being a monkey, swinging idly through the trees and living a quiet existence in the depths of a jungle- a very active and sometimes perilous one, to be sure, but a relaxed one, in essence, far away from the trappings of city life.

But now as he beheld these creatures on this day, even they seemed to carry a certain mysticism, a certain magical sense in their forms. He felt deeply connected to them; for he, as Parashuram's son, had some of the blood of Vishnu in him, and the Lord Hanuman was the greatest devotee of Lord Ram, the third avatar of the deity.

But as time went on, part of him faded. It seemed like there was an ethereal sense to it all; as if the flowing garments and battle scars and black axe of his father, the turquoise top and cascading hair of Ira, were but whisps of wind, illusions, like mirages in the desert. Every time he felt this, he strained to keep them there, but whenever he wished to go nearer to his father, something held him back, like the reluctance of a lost wanderer in a desert to go too close to a mirage, lest he find it to be a hallucination.

He felt in his core that something was wrong. Something was missing. Sorely missing. All this talk of gods and a quest was fine and hadn't failed to excite him and stir his soul with wild dreams of adventures and the bliss that lay at the end of it all. But part of him just didn't want it. Sure, his fate was unique. There was no other Kalki in the world. But maybe his mind, programmed over all these years to think like a mortal, just wanted a normal life.

Maybe the speed at which they were walking, at which his legs were working as if he was a superhuman, for unnaturally long periods of time, was making him feel rather uncomfortable.

He rushed up to Parashuram.

"How are we walking so fast? Shouldn't we be tired by now?"

Parashuram looked at him and didn't seem to pick up the state of flux his son's feelings were in.

"We are scions of Lord Vishnu," he said, his back straightening and muscles flexing in pride. "For us, no distance is too long; no task is insurmountable. The mortal body is constrained by fatigue, by limits to its endurance and capability. Not so for us."

He raised his hands to cradle Abhay's head in between them, applying a gentle touch, as if seeking to calm and warm him. But they felt cold, almost frostbitten. Abhay flinched, and Parashuram withdrew his hands, puzzlement glinting in his eyes, but also the beginnings of a sudden flash of fear fluttering in there.

"What happened, son?"

Abhay didn't understand what happened next.

It felt like the curtain of the mirage was pulled back, and the midday sun broke through. His skin felt scorched, his dry tongue parched with thirst and hunger. He'd never walked for this long in his life before. His skin turned pale, and his legs seemed suddenly fragile like the stems of reeds, wobbling as he leaned on his father for support. His head seemed to blur over; then there was a vision.

It was night. Pure pitch-black night. At the center of it, a golden wheel of innumerable spokes in concentric circles, and lit ghostly yellow-orange, spun. The outermost spokes were toothed and sharp like piercing blades as they cast shafts of light into the air. But these shafts, starting with a deep yellow color, dimmed until they were gray.

Then the whole wheel turned into a nebulous circular mass, at first haloed by and then engulfed by an ashen, gray shadow like primal cosmic dust. Then out from the mist came a solitary blade; a broadsword, with a sickeningly thin point reached by the convergence of a mass of cold steel…steel? Or some celestial metal, mined from the depths of the sea or the cores of waning, dying white dwarf stars? Who wielded it?

He felt his father let go of him, as a chill ran up his spine and fear towered before him.

Rimmed against the pleasant neon green landscape and the misty distant hills, was a vast shadow.

The red eyes glowered down at him like blood moons, a mass of emerald green hair billowed from it like a nest of serpents. The nose was a wolf's snout, the chest was an artwork of scars and gashes, and the body was an occult hoard of golden rings, bangles, and necklaces.

Two sharp silver fangs jutted from his mouth like icicles, and those teeth seemed to drive shafts of cold into his heart and felt like the same cold he'd felt in his father's face, in his heart, the source of that stale feeling that had tinged the air since morning.

His heart skipped a beat.

It was the same beast from the previous night. The broadsword from the vision was there. The feral eyes and lupine nose bristled, and he lifted his sword to cleave Abhay's neck.

It never reached its target. Through the air, swung the crescent axe of Parashuram. It smashed into the sword, and there was a reverberation, deeper than the clang of metal, nay, deeper than the hammering of an asteroid into the Earth, or than the explosion of a star.

Parashuram's dark form glowed, shining all over with a brilliant, deep light, as if the radiance of the Sun was diffusing into his bones. His eyes blazed with flame, and in them Abhay saw the wheel again, spinning furiously against a midnight-blue backdrop colored by nebulae and galaxies. Memories returned to him, memories of a tale he'd read of, when the Kaalchakra, the wheel of time, spun, determining the fates of mortals and gods, of worlds and ages.

Abhay was transfixed in terror as it arose in him,

a sharp pang of realization; this was not the battle of Parashuram and some anonymous demon. This was the battle of the Lord Vishnu and the hordes of darkness. And he, despite supposedly being Kalki incarnate, was helpless to do more than watch.

The beast snarled. He lifted his black hand, and Abhay could see the strength of the finger joints, fastened together in a clenched fist, with the power of destruction packed in that mass. He swung it at Parashuram and rammed it into his face, as the solid form of the god was turned into a blur of flailing limbs and flashing eyes. Then he was there again, a few feet away, a palm on the floor and his feet planted firmly, eyes burning brighter than ever. His other hand still grasped the handle of the axe. In his arms, the veins swelled, throbbing rivers of blue flame; his mighty muscles surged in their seats of skin like warriors arising from their thrones to join the fight.

All this strength gripped the axe, and then swung it upwards in a flowing curve like a rising wave. It stood there, a weapon so infused with power, with divine might, with the pulsing, racing vigor of life and of nature, a blade like the dark side of the moon.

Then the moon came somersaulting like a shooting star at light speed at the monster. But he was quick, despite all his colossal bulk and mass, and like a whirlwind, he stepped away from the line of fire.

However, he was not quite quick enough. The axe

tore asunder his arm from its joint, severing it. One dark, hideous mass of flesh fell to the floor.

The beast screamed; a guttural cry of wrath, primal and deep, the force of his rage exploding from his chest in shockwaves that blasted upon Abhay's already wild mind and frail ears, bearing down upon him and forcing him into a kneeling position, contorting himself into a ball, in a vain attempt to find refuge.

His head spun; his eyes dimmed, consciousness fading under the weight of a force from another world, a mere glimpse of the power held in the hearts of the world-wrecking beings of malice his tiny planet reckoned with. The same golden wheel from before rotated interminably, like a hypnotic pendulum, and all the streams of his thought and emotions flowed right into the center of it.

His mind spun with it, in a revolutionary dance into the night.

***

For Ira, all was chaos; the world was a frenzy of madness, of blood, of shadows prowling, of wild battle and death.

She grabbed at her head, already fading into the darkness as she sank onto a bed of moist grass that seemed to be painted all over with tears, a sea that would engulf her and reduce her to a pitiful shade of sorrow.

Something told her she should do something. Something told her she should fight. Something told her she should search in the mayhem of her mind for her mother and heed her words.

But all those voices went silent; her brain went numb. Numb with terror, numb with disorientation, numb with…numbness, as if she'd been drugged and reduced to a paralyzed, delirious state. For before her was something she had never imagined in her wildest nightmares.

Not like a demon from a typical horror film, but something deeper; something conjured by the most insidious sorcerers of the spectral realm. Not a phantom, not a ghost; but a real being who had the power not just to evoke blood-curdling, spine-chilling fear, but to kill.

A towering form with black hair like a tempestuous sea, thrashing in the wind. A single dagger, no bigger than Ira's palm, but with metal that shone deep black, with evil, serrated edges.

Her body, a nebulous form of shadow, was robed in some flowing garment like a sari, said the still-sane edge of Ira's consciousness. But it too kept billowing in a blur. The green in it was like the boughs of trees moving in the gusty wind. When she looked deeper, beneath the surface, she saw a lighter, yellowish green, like the conical, rounded fruits of a small *soma* plant, seated lightly on the branch of a tree…

She paused. Why was she thinking like this?

Ira, follow me, and you will live, and triumph.

It was her mother. Her voice was no more the wispy, enchanting tone of an angel, but now the urgent tone of a mother, who sensed her daughter in danger. Suddenly, Ira's senses flicked a switch. The fog in her vision was cleared; her ears were unclogged; her mind was emptied, until she was gazing straight on, not at a nameless demon, but at one of her kind.

The name of this creature came to her. Her unkempt hair, her sari, which seemed more woven from the soil and leaves of the Earth than spun from fabric, the sweet smell and yellowish-green fruits of *soma*, the magic herb of healing and rejuvenation; minor details that now were furiously analyzed by her mind, adding up to create a clear picture. The being herself seemed in slow motion, as if frozen by the forces of illusion, of *maya*, in a tableau so that Ira may gaze into those deathly black eyes and ancient form and glean from them not terror but understanding.

Ira felt as if her mother wasn't speaking to her; she was merely setting Ira's soul free with some magic, to row through the eternally flowing streams of Maya's consciousness. A reservoir of memories, thoughts, knowledge, and secrets that were born in the depths of time, filled with legends and stories and myths with a scale that bewildered. Then she stopped at some point on the stream, dropping her oars and dismounting. These weren't myths. They were snatches of life, glimpses from another time, a time that was too distant, too shrouded by forgetfulness, incubated from oblivion only by the dusty pages of the Vedas- and the powers that remained from then.

This is Jara. She is an Asura manifested on this Earth as a woman of medicine, of healing. I know her. She possesses drugs, and medications, brewed deep in the forests where her spirit dwells, and with those she has addled your brain and is possessing you before she slays you.

What do I do now?

Ira asked her mother, the voice of her mind rising up in panic as the unsheathed dagger of the Asura, slow-moving though it was, seemed to pierce her mind like a needle.

Conjure.

Then Ira shut her eyes. All was darkness. But not one of fear. One of peace, one of quiet, one of tranquility, like the deep darkness of the cosmos. In that emptiness, there was nothing, but she found space for something that had been so lost, so far astray in the physical world where her mortal instincts saw only imminent death:

Herself.

In that instant, she felt the core of her soul pulsate, like a pulsating star; she felt a stirring inside her, her heart thundering at breakneck speed, her lungs filled with a new, intoxicating, fresh wind that flowed through her body and gave life to her spirit. She was again that girl at the window, beholding the crashing waves and cascading rain on Juhu Beach, but she was also so much more.

There were flashes in the darkness, like the streaking of a silver shooting star, like the shining of the gray Heaven's firmament.

What do I conjure, Ma?

There is but one thing that can transfix all in fear, in sudden stillness and remembrance, as the brain struggles with the sudden return of age-old memories and the deeply buried emotions that infused them. If you have the power to make people look at the darkness behind them and bring that into the present, they will crack and, for fear of breaking, bend to you.

Ira opened her eyes. She saw the dagger's blade a few inches from her. On its glinting blade, it felt like she saw the answer, scored in the pictographic script from the tablet: a single wheel of many spokes, that spun as the dagger ponderously came through the air.

She had never seen it before, but she knew, in her heart, what it represented. What she needed now was but one section of that, one fragment of the Wheel of Time and existence:

The past.

Then there it was.

A forest wreathed in sunlight. An elderly woman in a green-brown sari in the mossy, cobweb-infested interior of a cottage, is holding a cup hewn crudely from wood, and pouring a smooth, jet-black, shimmering liquid.

On a wooden cot before her was a tangle of rounded joints and blood; she caught snatches of chubby cheeks, knees, shoulders, and a stomach, but they were all disjointed as if cut apart. She saw the liquid flow onto the cot like a waterfall, gently, until its remnants dripped out of the empty cup like honey.

Then there was a king; a king clad in golden garments, bedecked with rubies and diamonds and various other precious stones, standing with pride behind white horses on a chariot, gazing into the distance. Then the skies turned black; there was a moon in the sky, nearly full but with part of the side faded out, shining with ghostly radiance. The wheel was there again…but not as a wheel. As a disc. A divine weapon that blazed with the flame of a supernova as it fell through the sky and sliced the king's head clean off, trailing blood and fire in the night, before stopping some way beyond its target and soaring in a clean arc back whence it came.

Then the night of the skies set, engulfing the land and shrouding all in darkness.

Ira's eyes opened. She looked back not into lidless black orbs, but very human eyes, wide with fear, face pale with anguish, mouth hung in shock. Her back was bent, her skin a patchwork of wrinkles, like a weary old woman.

She spoke.

"Who are you?"

Then Ira spoke. This time, there was no Maya- no mother, no illusion. Just her voice.

"I am Ira. Daughter of Maya."

She spoke. "I am Jara, daughter of Kali. I know your mother well; she's family. Only one of her brood could possess such power of illusion, of magic."

She gazed into the distance, her eyes blurring with tears and face coloring over with the mist of nostalgia. "He was a young boy, the heir to the throne of the ancient kingdom of Magadha. Born in two halves, he was cast out by his parents and realm; left to die. But I, with a more peaceful inclination than many of my kind, had taken house in the forest, and mastered the art of healing and the lore of herbs. I healed him with the drink from the fruit of the plant *soma*, the foremost in powers of healing. I joined the two halves, and he became, within a day of returning in one piece to his kingdom, King Jarasandha.

"Then," she said, her face darkening, as she looked down, as if afraid to look at the heavens, "He came into conflict with Krishna. Krishna killed his son-in-law, and he set out on a quest of vengeance but was constantly thwarted. Then Jarasandha fought on the opposite side of Krishna in the War of Kurukshetra, but Bhima slew him."

She looked down, her eyes closed.

"Thus, I, having healed a villain, became condemned by the Devas. They ordained that my name, *Jara*, be given a new meaning: decay, for nothing but suffering had stemmed from me". Her voice bit with sarcasm like piercing frost.

"So, what cause did I have to side with them? Against my own brother? No, I am loyal to the Lord Kali, and none shall shake me from that course. He has sent me here- to kill you."

Ira saw Jara's eyes throb and thin, until they were black slits. She saw, somewhere in their depths, a spark of flame. The dagger stirred again, as the grip around its handle strengthened.

Her voice was deeper now. The form of the old woman was gone, replaced by the ravenous, ruthless rasping of the enraged Asura. "And you, an Asura by blood, are in league with one of Vishnu's progenies, of Krishna's lineage! You would defy your family, falling for the tricks of your disgraceful mother and that *sanyasi* Parashuram! You..."

Then the *Parashu,* Parashuram's mighty axe, whistled through the air and cut off her head. Ira looked down now, and met the glazed, deathly pale eyes, before the body crumbled into dust.

***

Abhay felt the soft tickle of grass stirring in the wind on his back. He felt the cool touch of rainwater on his face and opened his eyes to see the marks of water all over his t-shirt, with some fairly fresh raindrops glistening on his arms. The air was pleasantly cool like of the sort experienced in the dusk between summer and monsoon, like the evening between day and night for Mumbaikars.

The skies were silver-gray, with a shining backdrop to the thick, bleary, dark gray clouds that stretched across the sky like the footsteps of some great cosmic elephant.

He lay on a hill and saw at his feet endless forest stretching into the distance, all the trees ablaze with a brilliant, neon-green flame, flourishing in the rains.

There were recollections on the edge of his mind, of his father, of guttural screams, of a flying axe. He strained to bring them back, so that he may remember where he was in time, now that he was lost in the space of a monsoon-fed remote forest.

Then a head lowered itself into Abhay's vision. It was Parashuram. Abhay started as he saw a scar near his lips throb a little as they curved out in a smile.

Then he looked down at Parashuram's body and saw another gash, all across his torso. He remembered the sharp, hefty broadsword, and shuddered.

"Are you fine?"

He leaned forward and embraced him. "Come on, son," said Parashuram, wrapping his arm around Abhay's back and leading him forth from the hillside. Not for the first time, it felt like he was calling Abhay 'son' rather than by his name because his heart found a quiet joy in the pleasure of talking to a child of his, after spending millennia alone.

"Much has happened in your absence."

As they strolled through the trees, striped squirrels scurried through the trees, bolting up and down branches. Abhay was startled to see, with upper body muscles bulging out of a solid, colossal frame, a Gaur, with a thick skull from which curved two horns, tough as iron.

They came to a clearing where Ira sat. As usual, she was fidgeting with her nails as she looked at the horizon, her lips moving quickly as if she was talking to someone. When she heard Abhay and Parashuram approach, she turned around and smiled. As she faced them, Abhay saw something new in her, a sense of peace, a sense of self-assurance. She seemed to recline a bit; her hands placed on the ground behind her. Her hair was not wild and unkempt, as it sometimes could be, but flowing like thick rivers, curving like the shapes of hundreds of *Parashus* had been woven into it.

Her hair was parted just enough to reveal eyes that seemed to shine with the beauty of hope, but also were still and calm, with the boldness of triumph.

"Hi," Abhay said.

"Hi," she said. Then her face colored with concern. "Are you fine?"

"Yes," he said. He noticed her smile as she gazed

again into the distance.

"What happened?"

She laughed. "You missed a lot, Abhay."

And over the next few hours, as the three sat down there upon a rather moist, mucky, bed of mud, not caring for the fate of their already filthy, partly torn clothes, many tales were told.

***

A few hours later, night had fallen. Abhay and Parashuram sat together in front of a blazing, crackling flame, burning on a hearth of wood Parashuram had gathered for them, casting a deep orange radiance into the midnight-blue sky. Ten or so stars twinkled, and Abhay gazed up at them in wonder, his face illuminated and imbued with the warmth of the fire. He'd never seen so many stars back in Mumbai. Then again, he'd never met an avatar of Vishnu who turned out to be his father, Asuras sent by Kali, a prophecy saying he'd save the world…he was in a new world.

But for the first time, as he beheld the immensity of the heavens, he felt dwarfed by it all.

Sure, he'd been shocked. It changed everything. But having experienced this world for a day, he felt lost. Lost amidst the heroism of his father, slaying a demon that was essentially the primal manifestation of darkness, whose presence numbed Abhay. Lost amidst the wizardry of Ira, who'd taken all of five minutes to learn the art of illusion-conjuring from her mother, and with it had held off, for ten minutes, a dagger-bearing Asura lusting for her blood, who turned out to be her mother's sister.

Everyone was in their element. Everyone had girded their loins, strapped on their swords, and readied for war…everyone other than him. It felt no more understandable to Abhay than when he'd read those vague, clichéd phrases in adaptations of old epics for kids.

Parashuram looked at him and placed his hand on Abhay's shoulder. "What's wrong?"

"Ira has so much power. All that magic, illusion. I have nothing. I may be your son, but I don't seem to have any of your courage, any of your righteousness, any of your strength. When that monster appeared before me, twice, in the forest and today, I was frozen. This numbing fear took over my system, and I could do nothing. I feared…I didn't even fear death. I feared…those eyes, those fangs, that sword. He put me in a trance, and all I knew was terror. He'd drive me crazy; I see random visions, of a golden wheel or disc spinning, and when I passed out, it was like I followed it into the darkness."

"And now," he said, tears beginning to stream down his face, "It feels like I don't want this. I…just want to be home. Back in Mumbai. With you of course," he added, reaching out and holding Parashuram's hand. "I know I'm being selfish and cowardly, but I don't think this is for me. I'm…scared."

He hung his head, not in the pointed way of people who just want to avoid the other's gaze, but in the bereaved, resigned way of those who are burdened, whether by sorrow or shame or exhaustion.

He felt a warm touch on his chin. Parashuram wiped the tears off Abhay's face.

"Do you know what that monster's name is, Abhay?"

Abhay shook his head. His gaze was still inclined downwards, but he tilted his eyes ever so slightly to meet his father's gaze, which was now warm, soft, and comforting, with the light of love and care shining so painfully bright in his eyes.

"*Bhaya*. Fear."

A cold filled Abhay's throat again, as if that frigid sword had been pressed right to it. Parashuram reached out with his right hand and placed it on Abhay's chest, as if to ward off the blade.

"Asuras are not mere physical beings. They are manifested only by either conscious effort and magical prowess or the thoughts, imaginations, or indeed, fears of other creatures.

When you awoke in the forest, you were afraid of the night; fear came out of the shadows to meet you. Today, your heart harbored doubts, and you were scared of your destiny; fear came to slay you."

Abhay felt rage burn within him; at himself. How frail, how spineless could one be, how devoid of courage, to have so much fear that it could create a monster to rival Parashuram in combat?

Parashuram saw this on his son's face; his clenched jaw, his narrowed eyes, and skin reddening as if stoked with coal. He leaned forward, and Abhay felt his tumultuous, raging smothered in an embrace. He exhaled deeply, letting out all his fears, and buried himself in his father's arms.

"We all have demons, my son. All of us are haunted. But we may find comfort, we may find refuge, if we seek it."

"I love you."

"I love you, too."

After a few moments, they came apart. Abhay smiled, and felt a warm glow arise in him and suffuse through his bones and skin. Parashuram saw it illuminate his face, giving off an aura of contentment and happiness.

"I find refuge in you."

Parashuram smiled.

"And I do in you, Abhay. Thousands of years of wandering, of war, without end…having you after all that is everything to me."

"But you need to find that fire within you too, Abhay. You need to discover that flaming core that is your true self which will burn on no matter how cold or dark it is in the world," he pronounced, and as his voice gained in depth and gravity and the flame flickered and shadows danced on his face, Abhay perceived that, for a moment, before him stood not Parashuram, but Lord Vishnu himself.

"All of us have an *atman* in us- our self, our soul. This is who we are. This is what we are."

Abhay heard these words, but while they flowed like divine music into his weary heart, his mind wouldn't listen fully. "Isn't myself just a muddled combination of all my emotions, all my thoughts, all my fears, all my desires, all my shortcomings?"

"No. Those are all in your head. All figments of your imagination, all things you can make and unmake at will if you master your mind. Most of them will be fickle and change with the exultations of victory or the travails of hardship. They are part of our *jiva-atman*, your ever-evolving self. But there is something at the center of it all, no matter how deeply buried or shrouded in storm clouds of fear or ignorance: your soul."

"And you, Abhay, are unique. There is no one in this world like you; the blood of Lord Vishnu runs in you, and unimaginable depths of power in your soul. If Ira has *maya*, you have true *shakti*. You," he said, pausing and looking deep into his son's eyes to emphasize his point, "Could wield this *Parashu* far better than I ever have. Indeed, you could wield much deadlier weapons. You have a special purpose, a special destiny; for you are fated to save the Universe from annihilation. You are Kalki. There has never been a more important manifestation of the Lord on this Earth."

Abhay felt the power; he felt the energy from Parashuram flow into him, the undying faith. But all these prophesies, these promises, these hopes of him being an invincible savior, only made him feel smaller. Was he then so frail that he couldn't appreciate or use that power? But he remained silent and Parashuram saw his gaze drop again.

"Let me tell you something, you were afraid of being alone in the wild in the forest; you were afraid of facing your destiny in the fields. But you did not *fear* them. Fear is a much deeper, much more insidious emotion, of which these are but manifestations. These manifestations are glimpses of that darkness of fear, the darkness that festers and rules at the back of your mind."

For a moment, Abhay saw a flash of a blade in the air behind him, and the brief glow of two red eyes. He closed his eyes and willed them to go away. They did.

"The wheel…"

"The wheel is the *Sudarshan Chakra*, weapon of the Lord Vishnu, but also a symbol of the wheel of time, the Kaalchakra, the cycles of birth and rebirth, the *yugas* of creation and destruction and war and peace of our world. Your visions of that represent another manifestation of your fear: the fear of time. For we are in the *Kali Yuga*, the age of darkness, and thus our endeavor to deliver this tablet," he said, lifting it, with its assemblage of pictographs, next to the fire. "We face peril and threat. You fear that. You fear for your life, for your grandfather's life. But this is not the ultimate source of your fear," he added, as he thought he saw a false understanding dawn on Abhay's face. "This is but a symptom of it."

"Why is this fear there?" he asked.

"Because you allow it to be. To attain even a semblance of *moksha*, which is inner peace and the liberation of the *atman* from constraints, you must banish it."

"How?"

Parashuram smiled. "Do not fear the world. Fear your fear of it."

Abhay was still for a moment, dumbfounded. Then he laughed, his breath, held for the entire conversation, now coming out in a hearty display of delight and amusement.

"So, to get over fear you need fear?"

"In a way, yes."

Abhay looked up at the stars, and they no longer seemed to be ghostly, but bright and pure in all their beauty. Everywhere, there was an explosion of color, from the fire on the hearth to the black crescent *Parashu,* glistening like a dark moon, and the pulsing muscles of Parashuram by the light of the flame.

Then there was another question.

"Father?"

"Yes, son?"

"Who is my mother?"

There was a silence then, as if it was Parashuram's turn to fade out and let his mind settle amongst the stars, wandering in a far land of dreams and memories that now sloshed around him in a sea.

Then he spoke. "Abhay, what do you see when you look at the sky?"

"It's like…an ocean. Deep blue, bathed in the distant light of billions and billions of galaxies. There is the moon and the stars."

"We are all of that ocean, Abhay. We are all pure consciousness, shimmering with our own cosmic, little lights; and our family, Abhay, is of the Lord Vishnu. I am his sixth avatar; your mother, Dharani, who was an avatar of Vishnu's wife, Lakshmi. You, as our son, are perhaps more truly the Lord incarnate than any being ever was."

"Where is she now?"

"Her fate was not to remain on this planet, but to dwell in the heavens; the Goddess manifested herself as a human for your birth."

Abhay looked up at him and felt it well up again; that belonging, that love, that warmth, found in family and in further realization of who he was. But Parashuram felt in his stillness and his gaze, that question linger.

"She is in *svarga*, Abhay, watching on, watching

her son. I can feel her as I live, for she is not only my love but my being. Our bond is that of Vishnu and Lakshmi, older than the Universe."

Abhay felt complete as his father spoke, as if he could now at last sleep, sleep in a restful bliss and never get up, and join his mother where she was in the heavens. Part of him knew he would have to awake, that he had the purpose of his existence left to fulfil, but another part knew that as long as he had his father by his side, none of it would be anything other than blissful. This world was home, not because of the prophecy or his lineage, but because he had someone to belong with amidst all the tumult, who would love him and care for him like no one ever had.

Parashuram placed his son's hanging, sleeping head in his lap.

He didn't know if it was a dream, but as his eyes shut and his mind drifted to sleep, he saw Parashuram gaze at the tablet and mutter to himself.

"With the wings of wisdom, the pure white mane... and he'll need the blade too. The three possessions of Kalki. Trimbakeshwar, Trimbakeshwar...." The *Chiranjeevi* turned and gazed at the midnight-blue sky, as a sudden gust of wind blasted across his face. He paused, as if sensing Abhay was observing him. He merely smiled, still looking at the sky, as if gazing ahead at the future.

FIVE

Abhay awoke the next day. The fire had gone out in the cold of night, and he was alone by it. His head didn't rest in Parashuram's lap but on the motionless, stale grass.

Dark clouds wreathed the heavens like shadows shrouding the world from the light of dawn and smothering Abhay's breath.

Behind him, he heard hurried footsteps; but even they seemed faded, insignificant, like a lone, unheeded cry on a raging battlefield.

From the corner of his eye, he saw Ira. Her eyes were wide with fear, and her face had paled. Her eyes were red. A cry of alarm arose in Abhay for a moment. Ira raised her hands placatingly, and then Abhay saw the purple in her eyes, and the hair, not a flowing mass but a disheveled heap of strands strewn about her face. She had seen a sleepless night.

She moved her hands about, now one pointing, then the other beginning to count, but they were astray, conveying nothing except restless anxiety. At last, her mouth opened, and her glazed eyes lifted as they looked at something behind Abhay. She raised her right hand and pointed there.

Abhay turned. In the black clouds, forked shafts of white light miles long flickered and pulsated, before hammering upon the dark exterior of the clouds and wrecking the silence of the air with booms of thunder.

Gone was the impenetrable black sky. It was a tumult of winds howling, shadows shrieking and shifting. One raised a thick black arm and struck at another, the sheer form of a cold blade gleaming suddenly as it thrust for the kill. Then there it was; a pitch-black crescent beside a handle, a dark moon swinging in an arc through the sky. It was so primal in its manifestation of the cosmic night that it stood out even against the dark backdrop, absorbing all color and light. In it was the green of the trees, the blue of the peaceful sky, the white of the moon, the red of blood, the yellow of the sun.

Abhay felt his field of vision metamorphose from an abstract show of shadows to one of clarity. One of a muscular, raging champion of the Gods, a scar across his shoulder, dancing in the heavens like Lord Shiva, bringing his axe upon the skull of an abomination. A hideous monster of the night, with a fang and snout like a wolf and eyes like blood moons, gripping a great sword. It looked much like Bhaya, but Abhay knew in his heart that this was someone else altogether.

His heart was quiet as it beheld a duel between his father and the world-destroyer Abhay was meant to face one day: Kali Asura.

The axe clove into the skull of the beast, smashing into the thick mass of bone as if it shattered an asteroid, a sonic boom blasting through the heavens. But the cold shaft of the sword made contact and pierced through Parashuram's stomach. Then there was only silence; only a deathly pause, the pause of a soul as it fades from life to death.

Then they fell. Two giants; one with an axe embedded in his head, eyes and breath still; another with a sword thrust into his abdomen and jutting out from the other side. Parashuram's form was still the same; as he died, Abhay did not see his eyes turn pale, but wane with a new depth, like the depth of the Universe, shimmering with the light of another world. His face took on the peace, the quiet, the calm, with a gentle, knowing smile, that Abhay had come to love in his father.

Then the two beings were joined no more; it seemed to Ira that while the monstrous form of Kali kept plummeting into the Earth, into bottomless abysses and chasms of another realm, Parashuram came apart from him, floating away lightly, impassive even as the other hurtled to the Underworld.

Then the skies opened up. The darkness dissipated into dust, as if a curtain of blackness had been parted when Kali fell. A brilliant, white light, sheer in its brilliance, shone in its place, the firmament filled with a radiance. But it did not blind; it merely cast its rays of light across the forest and Abhay's body, as he was awash with the glow of contentment, of deliverance, of freedom.

Parashuram's body, hovering in the air, halted, as if held by celestial hands. Then there was a sound from afar; Abhay felt it come from a great distance, as if from heights beyond thought and time, transcending the Universe itself. But he felt it also louder than the claps of thunder, even than the primal bellow of rage and grief that was welling up in him at his father's death.

A conch, rending the firmament and sending its holy call across the world.

Abhay saw Parashuram's body wreathed in the light from above, the call of the conch becoming deeper and more thunderous until it reached a deafening crescendo. The Chiranjeevi's body shot up towards the light, before disappearing in it, swallowed by the heavens. Ira shielded her ears, but Abhay didn't care.

If the fires of hell were to raze him to ashes, if the blade of Kali were to eviscerate him to bloodied pieces, if a great wave were to rise and drown him in the deepest sea; he wouldn't care. He would take it all, though they would kill him.

For the dying found solace in the knowledge of rebirth, but the truly broken only despaired at the thought of a life spent mourning.

There was no heaven for him. As Kali had, he fell, dimly sensing a pair of hands hurrying to catch him but failing to stop him from thudding to the ground.

***

As Abhay came to, he was greeted with the ominous vista of dark storm clouds stretching to the horizon. The trees were silent and stale ghosts of dark green, like Abhay's soul.

His mind had throbbed and raged through hours of nightmares; not so much of heart-wrenching visions, but of unspeakable sensations; of the enveloping of his heart and form in a deathly cold, of being alone in the middle of the black depths of an ocean, of feeling his father's arms around him only for them to be charred and replaced by the ghastly body of Kali.

There was silence inside; just a dim but all-encompassing sense of emptiness, and he felt the welled-up anguish, the bereavement of loss, festering somewhere in its utmost depths.

Then there was a sudden feeling of warmth; of being smothered in thick, bushy hair like a blanket, with the form of another wrapped around him. It was not like the firm, mighty figure of Parashuram nor the aging, gentle frame of his grandfather, but the young, spirited form of Ira. In every inch of her skin, in every finger on her hand, in the pressing of her every bone on him, he felt life. He felt that vigor, that breath of passion, the kind that did not fear but reveled at the clapping of thunder, burst into his skin and began to dance in his soul.

He felt also a calming lull spread across him, like the feeling of one doused in an ice-cold bath after a scorching, parched day.

Then, slowly, Ira moved back, leaving Abhay seated there. The teary eyes and misty gaze and drained expression that had convinced Ira to give him a hug were gone. She could see from the depths of his eyes that he was troubled, but his face at least had begun to take on a semblance of peace.

Then he spoke, and while his voice was not choked with sorrow, it was hollow, with the kind of hollowness left after a person is separated from the one who gave them faith and the desire to live, a separation that congeals his lifeblood and strips away all his happiness in one stroke.

"We're done for, Ira. My father was our final hope. The world's end," he pronounced, his features darkening with foreboding, as if a great Asura loomed before him, "has come."

What should I do now, Ma?

Parashuram shall be resurrected if you two triumph.

But...said Ira, faltering as she paused before saying words she knew she wasn't supposed to say.

You will emerge victorious. The tablet will reach its destination. Then justice shall be brought to this world and all that you two have lost shall be restored.

Those words were spoken with such sheer finality, such assurance, that they were like spells on Ira's wild mind, taming it and setting it upon the path ahead.

"Abhay, if we complete this quest, your father will come back."

You idiot, she cursed herself, as Abhay's gaze lifted slightly before fading away again. This wasn't the time to talk to Abhay about the dangers of their mission and the fulfilling of an, to rational minds, impossible quest.

"But how..."

She didn't know what happened in that instant, but a small blaze was started in her, incinerating the phantoms of doubt and blazing away the demons of silence.

"We are Kalki, Abhay. You and I. Together." She reached out and gripped his right wrist tightly, and Abhay did not perceive the soft grip of a friend or a fellow lost soul, but the iron clasp of a warrior.

"This tablet," she said, reaching under the wood on the dead fire hearth and producing it, "has our world's fate written on it. If we deliver it to Mount Kailash, we win. We will be happy forever, with our loved ones back with us. If we don't, we will live the last seven days of our lives in despair at the impending apocalypse, which will end everything we know and love."

"It is a simple choice. Go forth or go back. Forward, there is the chance, however faint, however outrageously improbable, of victory. Behind, there is only a darkness, a cold regret that will eat away at our hollow, depraved souls till the day we are burned in the flame that consumes the Earth."

She pressed the tablet into Abhay's arms.

"Your father held this until yesterday. He braved the sword of Bhaya and the primordial wrath of Kali Asura to save you, to save us, and to keep the fight against darkness going for another day. But he wasn't Kalki."

"He was the guru of Kalki," said Abhay, distantly, remembering the conversations of another night.

"Exactly. He has taught you what he could, given you what guidance and strength he could in the time he had. Now it is up to you to take up the mantle."

Then Abhay felt it; he saw the hideous, murderous, accursed, filthy form of that *rakshas* and imagined tearing the tendons and bones of that body apart with his sword, leaving a trail of blood across the skies above Mount Kailash.

Ira shrank back as Abhay's jaw and fist clenched, his arm muscles tensing so much that dark blue veins ran through them like rivers of power.

He took his right palm and held the tablet with the strength that his father clung to his axe with, wrist so taut Ira thought it would snap, as it strained almost to break the tablet with brute force. Then the grip loosened, and Abhay looked back at Ira with bloodshot but blazing eyes, tapestries of deep, pained red and flaming, fierce fire.

This time Ira didn't shrink back. Something in her soul was awoken, stoked by that fire, by that vigor, by that unfettered hunger for vengeance and to throw oneself before the ravaging hordes of hell.

"Trimbakeshwar," said Abhay. This was not the faded voice of one in mourning, nor the trembling voice of a scared child. This was the assertion of one with clarity; one with a lucid understanding of his purpose, one who carries the blazing embers of his soul everywhere, to light his way in the darkest caves and most winding roads, and thus feared nothing. He recalled his father saying that word yesterday, and knew, somehow, as if it had been built into the fabric of existence by the Devas, what that meant.

"A *jyotirlinga,* 200km from here, housing a shrine of Lord Shiva. There, we shall find what we need to complete this quest."

He arose, gripping the tablet with his right hand, with Ira by his side, and strode forth to meet his destiny.

***

They walked. For hours they walked through the fields, through forests, sometimes seeing the suburban sprawl of small towns in the distance, with their little buildings stretching across a vast space, so different from the Mumbai they were used to. But then again, everything was so different. Abhay felt his legs pumping like they never had before, with a new strength in his soul, as if he was at last at peace with his powers and his identity as Kalki, and the son of Parashuram.

Whenever he stumbled, it was not due to fatigue, but due to a sudden remembrance of his father, a frame from the last night with him by the campfire, or when he'd first met him, emerging out of a portal of light in the forest – which, for a moment, stilled him, and sought to weigh him down with loss and despondency. He felt it at the edge of his consciousness; a nebulous, fermenting mass of grief and pent-up wrath; if he gave it entry, it would flood his mind and heart and overwhelm him. When this happened, he would lean on Ira, who would help him up, while whispering soothing words in a language he didn't understand. Maybe it was the language of *Maya*, of illusion, of magic, to bring rest to him.

Then he would look at the tablet and then see the entire stretch of his quest before him, all the way through fields and forests and sacred temples and deep lakes and to the feet of Kailash Parvat itself, towering in a freezing landscape of snow and rock. At the summit sat Lord Shiva; at the summit were the twin celestial lakes of the Sun and Moon; at the summit was the Gateway between Heaven and Earth, where they would complete their quest.

Maya spoke constantly in Ira's head, telling her of the directions when they needed it. She felt a change in the air today; sure, the loss of Parashuram grieved her too and made part of her fear the dangers ahead, but now, it was truly up to them. Kalki had been thrust into the limelight, and there was no going back. Perhaps death lay on the path ahead, but she was prepared to brave any perils as long as there was the smallest hope of bringing her father back.

Night fell on the plains. Abhay gathered wood and set them in the middle, as he sat down, allowing exhaustion to fill his bones and flow through them, thick like honey, making even the hard rock clearing feel like a comforting cocoon. In the day he'd been striding forth tirelessly like a god. But in the night, felled by sleep, soon to be lost in a vast dreamscape, he was human, and he found that he still treasured that.

He wondered where Ira had gone, and then saw her, bearing two cups of wood containing black liquid.

"What's that?" he asked. He didn't know why as he looked at the drink, sloshing in the starlight, glistening pure black, he felt something awake in him.

"*Soma,*" said Ira, handing him a cup and sitting down next to him. "Don't you notice how we haven't eaten anything since we left?"

"Oh, yeah," said Abhay, laughing, but also lost in thought as he gazed at the midnight-blue sky awash with stars. It'd been so long since he'd tasted anything on his lips. He lifted the glass, and intended to chug it in at one go, but as he put his lips to the liquid, he found his tastebuds throbbing in pleasure, and his mind filling with a glow of warmth, of bliss, of magic, like he was drinking stardust. Every drop of that substance felt like it had a little of the essence of the Universe in it, shining extra bright when he looked at it and seeping through his throat like space dust.

When he put it down, he saw that he'd only drunk a little beyond the rim of the cup, though it'd felt like he'd swam in an ocean of the stuff.

"I've...never tasted anything like this," he managed, holding the cup by the hearth, before realizing there was no fire on it.

"No fire today?" Ira said, voice accentuated by a question.

Abhay sighed, before looking down, that empty, pensive look taking over his face. "No Parashuram, no fire."

Then he heard something; a crackle, a sizzle, a burst of a spark. He looked up, and saw himself gazing into a wispy, blazing mass of flame like a nebula in space, hues of the brightest pink and the deepest, most flaming orange merged together in a beautiful color. It was still a small fire, but rose and ebbed a little every moment, like a beating heart.

He saw Ira extending her hands and controlling it, her eyes narrowed in concentration, and Ira could feel her eye muscles tensing, her palms stiff, as she mustered all her strength to create the fire.

At last, she let go, snapping out of that tableau of intense effort, and the flame flared up, like the core of a young star amplifying its blaze as it discovered new reservoirs of flame within it. Then it was there, waving in the wind, every molecule of its being imbued with a special radiance.

Ira leaned on Abhay, exhaling, as she watched, with tired but thrilled eyes, the completion of her masterpiece.

"How did you do that?"

"Oh, it's *maya*", said Ira, as she straightened. She twirled her fingers again and the fire dissipated into nothingness, and darkness returned, before spinning her wrist again and bringing it back.

"Did your mother teach you?"

"Teach? No, she didn't *teach* me to conjure fire," she said, shaking her head as she gazed with contentment upon her creation. "She taught me only to find the fire within myself, to unleash my powers of conjuring and magic. There is a fire within us, Abhay. You said 'No Parashuram, no fire'- that's wrong and undermines your potential."

They looked at each other, faces illuminated by the glow of the flame, and felt a new life, a new fervor, arise in them.

"Every day, I learn a new way of manifesting that power. Yesterday, it was reliving the past to open the floodgates of trauma and distress in a troubled Asura's mind; today, it is to give us warmth here on the plains."

"So, it's nothing? I mean," he said hurriedly, as Ira shot him a look of sudden offence, breaking the heavenly tableau of warmth they'd been locked in. "It's just...lights? And sound, of course, of the crackling and hissing. And the smell, of course, the thick smell of burning…" He trailed off, as he realized his mind couldn't distinguish, no matter how hard it tried, between that conjured flame and a real one.

"Our lives are illusions," said Ira. "My mother says that. Well, of course in a sense we do exist. But the meaning we assign to the sights and sounds and smells around us, to the people and landscapes and portents that influence us, is self-concocted, in our minds. Nothing physical carries any meaning on its own, it is just an assortment of molecules. So are we, just mixtures of neurons and hormones and bones and DNA. In fact, nothing in our minds means anything, it is our creation, how we choose to perceive the world."

"My father would say at this point that what has meaning is who we are," said Abhay. "Our *atman*, our souls, our true selves; and we need to free ourselves from the rule of our thoughts and desires to truly be at peace and unlock the *atman*'s potential. The *atman* lives on through death and takes on a new body and endures thousands of such deaths and rebirths."

Ira nodded. "Yes, our minds are fickle, and more superficial than we realize. Our souls are entirely different though. Hell, I can read minds."

Abhay shot her a look of alarm, and she laughed lightly; but not too lightly. "I know it sounds creepy, but that's just another thing I've picked up. I know, already, that the human mind is a chaotic place. I suppose being a human is enough to find that out," she continued. "I mean, all of us are crazy, confused, restless beneath the surface, always longing for something more but not knowing what we want. But these past few days," she said, looking Abhay in the eyes, "have taught me this on a new level."

Abhay saw her eyes darken, and though she didn't move, her frame shifted, inclined away from him.

She saw Abhay look away too, at the stone ground, and in that moment, the fire on the hearth seemed to fade away just a little. At last, Ira subsided. Abhay saw her uncertain gaze soften into one of questioning, the kind of puzzled look we give when unable to understand the behavior of our friends, or those we love.

"That day, when we got the tablet on the cliff, you...*growled* and said 'she is an asura'. Over the past few days," she continued, voice gaining strength as she continued, "I've seen it in your mind. Respecting your privacy, and also given my beginner-level skills, I haven't seen even the smallest fraction of your thoughts and emotions. But any in which I was involved stood out to me. Sure, there were some positive emotions," she said, part of her trying to lift Abhay as he continued gazing impassively at the ground, "but there was also… *fear*. Distrust. Even a sense of…." she shuddered as she remembered the sharp pang of it, like a cold blade, "hatred." Abhay winced, and she felt as if she'd jabbed him with a blade herself. But she pressed on. "Why?"

Abhay was silent. His thoughts wandered in that moment from the image of Parashuram, speaking with awe of the Lord Vishnu, to a vision of Mount Kailash, abode of Lord Shiva. He thought of the heavens, their heights, their glories, their greatness. Then he thought of the darkness. He thought of Bhaya, seeking to tear him apart in the forest, with those fangs and blood-red eyes. He thought of Kali Asura, who'd slain his father, and felt part of his spirit sink again into that mire of mourning and grief, before rising up again. His mind cleared, and he turned to face Ira, and then began to walk away.

"Oh," she said. She nodded briefly. Immediately, like a lost soul at sea searching for a lighthouse, she reached out to her mother in silence.

Ira, it is natural for one with Asura blood to clash with one of Deva blood. It is built into him, that genetic strain of Asura-hatred, over generations in which his ancestors have warred with our kind.

Why don't I feel hatred for him then?

Because as my daughter, as one whose blood is imbued with an understanding of maya, your heart understands that all these notions of light vs dark, all this generalizing and classifying of celestial beings into two halves based on the deeds of a few, are illusions, narratives forged over the millennia by the victors, by those who would raze all evidence of the other side being capable of virtue.

Ira listened. She looked at Abhay's troubled face and at the skies, grasping for words.

Then she did something Abhay had not expected; after all, *he* would be insulted and furious if he saw, in the mind of a friend, disrespect and resentment for his heritage. But she didn't raise her voice; she didn't walk away.

Abhay noticed some movement on the periphery of his vision and neglected it at first. But it kept coming closer, slowly breaking through the thick shroud his mind and body were wreathed in. He finally stared right on at the source of this motion as a hand, glowing by the firelight, shining with beauty and the tenderness of heartfelt approach, touched his shoulder. Behind it, the form of Ira, silhouetted against the blaze, came closer.

It was a reassuring touch, as if seeking to stroke away the demons from Abhay's skin, as she rested a bit on his shoulder and looked into his eyes.

"Abhay," she said, wrapping her arm around his back, as Abhay found his body swathed in warmth and softness. Hesitantly, he turned around and faced her.

"We are in this together. No matter what history lies

between our people, no matter what old sages or even the heavens would say about what a Deva and Asura should do to each other. Yes, my people have spilled Deva blood, including some with genes you carry in yourself. Your ancestors have slaughtered mine too. But ask yourself, what is more important to you? That blood, or the blood of your grandfather, ripped open by Kali's sons? Or the blood of your father, Parashuram, shed when Kali Asura thrust that sword into his heart?"

Abhay did not even flinch as he looked right into her eyes, and the nightmarish memories of the past few days raged somewhere in the background, a mass of rising waves that could flood him any moment.

But she looked away and gazed into the deep-pink-orange depths of the magic fire, as its sparks danced in her eyes and cast their radiance across her face.

"Or the blood of my father, his throat cut in the doorway of my bedroom?"

A silence hung there, and Ira nearly saw them; ghosts swaying with the flame, specters raising their cold shadow as the trauma of loss returned, fresh in the minds of the young victims.

Then she spoke again, and they dissipated.

"We have both lost those we loved the most," she said. "And to avenge that loss, to war on for this grief and loneliness that binds us, we must push on and forgive these ancient sentiments." Strong words, Abhay thought, as they tore into the night air and seemed to open up the scars in his soul. But they were right. And both of them knew that.

There was nothing to be said. Arms wrapped around each other, they looked up at the heavens, and watched the full moon, complete now and casting its pure, pale radiance across the plains.

At last, Abhay spoke.

"Remember when we were enemies in school?"

"Oh yes," said Ira, laughing heartily. "I don't think I ever told you," She said, her face assuming mock seriousness, "but I hated you. Who did you think you were, some god, that you knew everything and could lecture the whole world about it?"

Abhay mimicked her face and saw her smile just a little. "I hated you more. Who did you think you were, flaunting your long, scruffy hair and sports medals everywhere?"

They guffawed this time, rolling in hysterics on the grass and holding on to each other so they wouldn't burst apart.

"Scruffy was just too much," said Ira.

"Yeah." said Abhay.

As they looked at the stars, something dawned on him.

"I think we were who we are the whole time."

"What do you mean?"

"You were an Asura. Wild, restless, riotous. I was… my father's son. Always taking myself seriously, seeing visions that made no sense to me..."

"Well, we've been who we are our whole lives; and we will be, till the day we die. Our destinies were written for us long before we were born."

"Now," she said, glancing at the tablet, on whose surface danced the pink and orange of flame and the midnight-blue of sky and the white of moonlight, "We just have to fulfil it."

***

After they awoke at daybreak, they kept marching on, Maya guiding them through valleys and across rivers. There were few words after all the talk of last night; only a constant state of travel and toil, striding towards their destination.

At last, as they walked through a vast forest, they found themselves moving up the slope of a hillock. Abhay knew, somehow, that he'd be in sight of the place soon. As they reached the top and stood in a few feet of tree-free space, they saw it.

A three-faced black conical spire stood raised up higher than eye level. Its substance was smooth like silver, but Abhay felt as if embedded into its form was an old fire, as if the rocks of a volcano had been molded and welded into this building. At the peak was a single golden orb like the sun, atop a few steps of shining metal.

"We have reached," announced Abhay.

He rushed down the hill, and Ira followed him.

They shoved through a few feet of forest, racing through the bushes in a primal blur of thrill and anticipation; for the wonders that lay in wait, for the magical feelings that would flow through them in the *mandir* of a primordial being that transcended the Universe.

As they finally breached the forest and skidded down a rocky cliff like the wind, they saw it: a structure, with the sable-black substance of the spire flowing and curving like waves of the night into two other hemispherical structures next to it. All of this merged into one form that stood out against the light of day like the moon in the night, like a blazing star in the blackness of the cosmos. Abhay did not know why, but he felt as if all the thoughts, emotions, and upheavals of the past few days evaporated as he approached the temple complex. All he had left was a single, pure river of flowing consciousness that seeped into every inch of the structure before gushing forth from the walls, fresher, infused with life, and filled with a sublime bliss.

They came to a brick wall that went up to their waist and leaped over it, placing their palms on the barrier as they sprung into the complex.

They stopped, the volcanic rock of the walls looming above them. In them were carved and chiseled many layers, so that the wall was like a tapestry of a multitude of folds, like a mountain by the sea sloshed by many waves.

Abhay felt, there, a profusion of visions. It wasn't that he *saw* them; but he felt them manifest on the edge and yet, at the core of his mind, nay, his being. A pure white crescent moon; the flashing of a three-pronged blade, with a central shard reaching for the sky, from it two others curving away like tendrils of flame, Lord Shiva's *trishul.* The blazing of a pillar of fire of immeasurable height, like a pure sheet of celestial matter suffused with the might of Mahadeva.

Then he remembered it; the black outline of the *Parashu* against the stormy sky; and he felt a oneness with the being who bestowed it upon his father, who had manifested as a pillar of fire at this exact spot in the depths of time.

He pictured it, not as a dreamed image, but a remotely viewed destination, which he perceived with the core of his soul. He surged forth. Ira followed.

Then he stood before it. He found it impossible to believe he was truly here, at a site where he sensed his fears would be conquered, his suffering lost like the ephemeral thing it was, his quest to find some meaning and strength. *No*, he corrected himself. His *mind* found it impossible to believe. But his soul knew he'd always been meant to come here.

He'd always been meant to stand before the pure, perfect form of Nandi, Shiva's mount, gazing on into the depths of another structure. He'd always been meant to feel everything gathering, assimilating into one mass, one thought, one emotion, as he looked at those depths.

A love for the Lord who reigned over it, who reigned over the whole Universe, who *was*, in essence, the whole Universe.

He strode forth into the darkness.

He was distantly aware of a structure before him, a shape, a Shiva-*linga* in which all pilgrims sought the love of and unity with Lord Shiva. But he needed it not.

He kneeled, and then sank, and then lay before it, his feet, knees, palms, chest, and forehead. He felt his body pulsate and vibrate on the ground, as it throbbed with a new, divine energy, shaking like the pulsing of a star. Then it was still; a heavenly stillness, as if his heart had flown, free, into the endless reach of the firmament; then into a space transcending everything, where only dwelt Shiva.

Then he felt it susurrate through his form, then through his soul; five syllables, sounds of power, vibrations, the essence of a cosmic energy, with time it sank more deeply into his being, which he felt to be one with the Universe and imbued with bliss. His palms joined and were unified in one body of worship and pure devotion.

"*Om Namah Shivaaya.*"

His soul rested there at that altar; not a physical

altar of stone or gold, but a celestial altar, where he prostrated himself before the feet of a primal deity in reverence and love. But he felt, dimly, like on a different, fainter, plane of existence, himself standing outside the structure, outside the darkness, and in the light of day.

There, he beheld before him a towering white horse; standing far taller than he, with a radiant form to humble the brightest star, chest and body glistening, with the light nestling itself in the ridges of great muscles. His face shone with a divine light and shimmered as if it had an aura of holiness, with blue eyes like the depths of the ocean, like the depths of the cosmic realm where Shiva and all souls dwelt. All along his neck was a white mane, billowing with vigor in the gusting wind.

There was also a green parrot, silhouetted against the blazing sun, beating its wings on the whispering wind.

Abhay's hands, still awash and infused with the bliss of prayer, were still together, but gripped a sword.

Its hilt was scored with runes, with marks of power that vibrated and emanated strength. From it, like the body of a river flowing from the mouth, came the blade; a narrow body, piercing as the third flaming eye of Lord Shiva, smooth and resplendent as Vishnu's *chakra*. For he perceived, along its edge and body, the wheel whirring on. The wheel of time and fate spun through the being of all of creation, but here, as Abhay moved the blade, he felt it pause in its revolutions, and spin the other way.

For he, this blade, his identity as Kalki, were all products of fate, realities churned by the thought of the Gods and the revolutions of the wheel, elucidated upon the surface of the tablet. Yet he also had in him a divine power to change fate, to save worlds, to determine the ebbing and flowing of creation and destruction with his sword and the strength of his will.

He would. He saw Ira laughing in joy at the deliverance of these gifts to Kalki, and smiled too, and felt his eyes open, breaking free from that state of deep contemplation, but still at harmony with his soul and with the cosmos.

He was not Abhay; a Mumbai teenager with the frailties of mortals, who had lost his father and grandfather in the past few days, thrust out into a Universe he feared.

He was the savior of worlds, the bearer of Vishnu's flame, Shiva's blessings, and Parashuram's power.

He was Kalki.

SIX

The next few hours were, to Ira, like a dream. The horse raced on like a shooting star, blitzing through rolling hills of granite, over vast plains rustling in the wind as if the earth breathed, and past cascading waterfalls.

She was seated behind Abhay, who seemed to know the horse, stroking its, no, *his*- mane, and whispering to him, seated erect as he rode, like a warrior.

Beside them flew the parrot, whose form seemed to emanate what her *Maya* instincts picked up as divine energies or the force of knowledge and wisdom. Indeed, as they approached evening when they came to the crest of a hill before a waterfall, she saw the parrot's form silhouetted against the water and felt it pulsate with a deep blue luminescence, like the pure, starry sky on a full moon night.

All around her seemed ethereal, incessantly stirring, glowing with magic and life. Once, she asked her mother, *who are these companions of ours? They will reveal it to you*, Maya replied, and Ira almost heard the smile in her voice, like the mirth of one who finds amusement in the possession of knowledge the other is oblivious to.

Night had fallen. The entire forest was a swarm of pitch-black trees silhouettes against the midnight-blue sky, shining with innumerable stars. The air was wreathed in blue as if they were swimming in an ocean. Every step was easy, yet almost too easy, and Ira felt herself wading through the magic that cleared the space before her and imbued all with a new, celestial beauty.

At last, they camped before a small hillock in the depths of the forest. She conjured another flame, and this time it blazed blue, merging with the backdrop of the forest, as if it was born from this landscape. While the previous day's flame had been unreal and flickering, this was deep, and in every flow of its curves and swirling of tendrils, she felt the flowing of waves in the ocean, that lapped on the shore of her soul and left it with the feeling of freedom, a new feeling of power, as if she'd been lost in this world the past few days and had finally found herself.

She observed the shining eyes of the horse, head

still raised as he surveyed his surroundings. Abhay had spoken to him and asked him to stand by the hillock. The parrot rested on his shoulder.

She saw the sword in his hands, glimmering in the night like a flaming star, blue sparks dancing across the blade like fireflies, the runes on the handle glowing like the letters on the tablet. She reached into her pocket and took it out. She had asked for it from Abhay, for she felt like it was only fair for the two halves of Kalki to share the responsibility.

Now, the tablet seemed to vibrate, as if picking up energy from the new arrivals, or perhaps from the Shiva *mandir* they'd just been to, emitting the pulsations to her hands, which convulsed and waxed flaming orange as she held it.

She sat down on the grass and stared into the fire's depths.

Abhay came and sat beside her.

"No *soma* today?" he asked.

"Oh...I forgot," she said, dazed, hearing her own thoughts come out in befuddled words.

He smiled as he saw her face and placed a hand on her shoulder. "It's ok."

Then it was there, in a flash. Her spine tingled, her mind fluttered, and her soul skipped a beat, but even she, the daughter of the cosmos' master of illusion and magic, was too slow. In front of the fire were two small cups of *soma*, the liquid sloshing as if someone had just placed it there and ran off, gleaming exactly like the previous night.

She looked up and found herself making eye contact with the parrot. Then it spoke- no, her mother spoke, returning to her hazy mind to stir it to action. *Drink it.*

She drank it. It was different this time, it wasn't a nebulous, magical feeling of bliss, but as if a mist was being cleared to reveal a new reality, her eyes picking up new vibrations, her mind picking up new movements in the air. She put it down and the parrot was right there, resting on her wrist, claws digging lightly into it.

"I am Shuka."

This wasn't her mother. Nor was this telepathy, or an illusion. This was true speech, though in a world where a horse, a talking parrot, and a sword appeared from thin air to answer prayers, words like 'true' didn't have much of a place.

"Hi Shuka, I am Ira...." She stopped. What was she doing? This was no pet, nor wild being. This was someone more. Someone here to give her tidings from the heartlands of the gods and illuminate the path ahead.

"I am Ira. Daughter of Maya. I am Kalki."

Shuka bowed his head in reverence, spreading his wings in courtesy and closing his eyes.

"Then know, my Master, that I see all, down to the depths of the past, through the hazy waters of the present, and up to the firmament of the future. There is much I could tell you, but first, you must ask."

She thought hard, straining to break free of all the noise of the past few days, all the magic and journeying and conversations, when the obvious struck her, and she berated herself for not thinking of it. For a moment, the old, logical Ira returned. *Gosh, Ira, what was your plan? I know this is a lot for you, but you can't be so spaced out that you have no idea where you wanna go. This isn't a movie!*

"Where…" she smiled as she thought of what'd just happened in her head, like old times. "Where to next?"

"A place sixty-nine yojanas south of here, in the hallowed, tree-nestled, blooming lotus lake of Pampa Sarovar. There rest primordial waters with immense power, waters that rage but also heal and purify. Near there is a hill with a *mandir*, where dwells one who will take you to Mount Kailash."

"Who is this?"

The parrot's beady eyes glassed over for a moment, as if for once departing from its divine flow of thought and entering the realm of memorization. "The one with lightning in arms, legs, feet, and tail."

Tail? thought Ira. *What…*she didn't feel like she had any mental space left to analyze that. The pronouncement of these tidings was more than enough. She looked down at the tablet and remembered it- "waters that rage"- a phrase Shuka used too to describe the lake. An indescribable sense of foreboding mingled with wanderlust kindled a primal fire in her soul, awakening her restless self. For now, she let that flame linger there, and asked something else that she found puzzling, now that the enigmatic Harappan pictographs danced in her mind as the letters recited by Parashuram.

"How…why…the *grhas,*" she said, at last. "The *mandirs*…how are they being destroyed?"

"They are being smitten asunder by the bolt of lore," said Shuka, and this time his eyes settled at a middle ground, where thought seemed to be brewing in their depths, but they gazed on into the horizon.

"The *vajra* astra," he said suddenly, as if someone on the horizon had permitted him to reveal this truth. "The weapon of Lord Indra, the king of all Devas, who reigns in Heaven, *Svarga*. This astra is among the most powerful in the universe, and appears as a bolt of lightning, but is infused with the energy of millions of them."

Ira had a flashback; she was standing on the hill beneath gray skies of thunderclouds, and seeing thunder rent the air and the flashes of lightning as Parashuram and Kali fought. It all made sense now. No wonder even the avatar of Vishnu hadn't survived; the charge and electric fire of a million lightning bolts had struck his heart.

Then she felt it; the presence of her mother, a being of cosmic energy and magic walking once more in her mind but treading with a certain tenderness as she intervened to grant her daughter a vision of the road ahead.

There it was. Standing, formidable in the faint sunlight breaking through the thick clouds and snow of the Himalayas, a cliff of rough, cragged rock, rimmed by snow. Upon it was a faint form, a faint outline. Ira did not know how to describe it; whether it had been carved into the rock by Shiva's trishul, or was merely a birthmark, born with it in the tumults of creation eons ago; she just knew in her soul that it was there.

A mark of two lines, curved at the edges, meeting each other in the middle, with four dots around their intersection. It had no color or texture, or, as Ira looked at it for a few more moments, even form. It was just *there*; just like her soul, which she couldn't see or easily feel, but existed at some deeper plane of existence. *The swastika*, said Maya's voice, ringing clear, echoing off the mountainside, but Ira felt as if it could also be her heart speaking with unexplainable knowledge, for this symbol was somehow scored into her memory, a memory of things she had never seen or consciously thought of before; perhaps a memory from those before her who had traversed this world, or from previous lives. *The symbol of the vajra astra.*

Then it went away as if blown away by a sudden chilly gust of wind, lovingly brushing against her mind and pushing her into the present. She was again in the midnight-blue darkness of the forest, before the parrot, whose brilliant blue eyes like sapphires were now fixed on her.

"The tablet," she said. She glanced at the text on the object again and determined to have a go at answering the most fundamental question of the prophecy. "How does that work? Why do we need to return it to the Heavens? Why would Kali Asura's possessing lead to the end of the world?"

The parrot inclined his head as if letting her quizzical words flow across his consciousness, churning them in the sea of his knowledge to unearth sacred answers. At last, he spoke.

Except he didn't. He didn't even tell her with his mind; Ira just knew what she had to do.

The letters on the tablet glistened and glowed golden, emanating that same magical aura and energy. But as she turned it over, she saw not the blank surface she expected, but a surface akin to that on Mount Kailash; it seemed rougher, more ancient, full of a primordial power. Then she sensed it in her mind's- no, her soul's eye- the swastika.

Shuka spoke.

"Any who obtain this tablet have mastery over the *vajra* astra. The Devas have many astras of their own, yes, some more terrible than the *vajra*. But they fear to unleash those on their offspring, indeed, on the extensions of their souls. Besides, that would commence a celestial war of apocalyptic proportions that could destroy their creation."

"Kali Asura and his forces are thus wreaking destruction with the astra, in temples, in the sacred places that are essential to preserving the light, the power of the gods, upon Earth in the Kali Yuga. However, the holiest of the shrines are protected by the power of the tablet. If he gets his hands on the tablet, he will be free to strike at the heart of the homes of celestial energy, starting with the *jyotirlinga* shrines of the Lord Shiva, one of which you visited."

"So, it's up to us," said Ira, gazing at the tablet as she never had. The fate of the world, and the designs of the gods, all rested on their shoulders. They'd never felt so heavy before; but nor had they ever felt so…*light*, sparkling with hope and a desire to complete this quest and brave all the dangers that stood in their path.

Shuka went silent. Then Ira opened her eyes.

The beady-eyed parrot stood on the horse's shoulder. Half the *soma* in her cup remained, still stirring and sloshing, the blue flame on the hearth reflected off the black surface. Abhay sat beside her, gazing pensively into its depths.

She saw his face, so serious, so still, and yet so restless, with brows furrowing and creasing and eyes waxing and waning, no doubt reflective of a mind that was wandering in far countries of dreams and ponderings. She resisted the urge to laugh as she contemplated for a moment what had just happened, while Abhay had been lost in his own world.

Abhay saw the devilish smile on her face, and felt the tableau of his concentration break, as he couldn't help but feel the tingle of the same thrill, the same rush. He smiled too, and Ira felt like a light lay on their path, on her and Abhay, that would never die.

But she guffawed inwardly at Abhay's stupefied expression and stutter as he tried to articulate. "What… did I miss something?"

"Quite a lot, my dear *Shiva-bhakt,*" she said, smiling.

"Well," said Abhay, looking at the parrot, as if he too was picking up strange signals from the bird, "We might as well get some sleep. We have a long day ahead tomorrow."

***

They awoke the next morning, the sun breaking through the trees and into their hearts, filling them with the warm glow of day, of hope for sallying forth into more danger and mystery, into their destinies.

Ira reached over and stroked the horse's mane. *Uthapati, Devadatta*, she thought, bidding him wake from his sleep. Not that he ever slept; he merely let his eyes close, riding through a world of dreams, while his senses continued to flow in the real world, prepared for sudden flight or to alert his rider to the presence of enemies.

She had gotten familiar with the horse the night before, and it turned out he had a predilection for telepathic Sanskrit, which was no problem to Ira, in days when she could communicate in pure thought with her mother an infinite distance away, in the heavens.

Abhay began to straddle the horse, placing his right leg, but Ira stayed him with a touch to his right palm. "Let me ride today," she said. Abhay assented.

She sat at the helm, and as the parrot beat his wings and began to take flight beside them, and Abhay started to hold on to her from behind, Devadatta pumped his leg muscles and flourished his flowing mane, and took a first, robust, stride. Ira felt not as if she was riding a horse but was on the front lines of an army. Then Devadatta took off, and they shot onward.

A dry, brown landscape of rolling cliffs and canyons blazed by, but Ira found herself not clinging on for dear life, but stretching her arms out, body open to the gusting wind, which seemed to pierce through to her spirit and stir up a storm of wanderlust and a desire to soar on through a world of endless possibilities and wondrous landscapes. The parrot flew by her, its form streamlined like a rocket as it hurtled through the air with motion as smooth as a glider.

At last, they rested by a narrow creek, gushing and flowing in a fluid channel that glistened in the sunlight, right next to another rocky, dark brown crag.

Abhay and Ira walked over to the waters to drink, but as they neared, the waters sloshed, as if tossed by some unseen wind, as if they were an ocean of their own, producing waves that broke and flowed and crashed in a world of their own. It seemed to Ira as if the water broke upon the riverbank, but left no indentation, no mark, no wetness that came with the touch of water.

Suddenly, it came back to her, a vision of her drinking *soma* the previous day. She didn't know why, but something deep inside her felt as if that magic, that celestial sparkle, had been stirred into this stream.

It also induced the same pause, the same hesitance from the frail mind, conditioned to think like mortals, before immersing itself in an intoxicating, heady world of heavenly tastes and senses.

Go on, Ira, her mother said. She walked on.

She joined Abhay at the bank, looking down into the waters, which seemed crystal clear, pure ultramarine as they shimmered in the sun, rays skipping off the crests of miniature waves, but yet not transparent, almost as if they were deceptive, concealing something dark beneath a veil of beauty and innocence.

She looked at her reflection and saw her whorls of hair unfurled into numerous streams across her face, blown apart by the wind and Devadatta's breathtaking speed. She seemed in her element; wild, free, and unruly, and she felt her face shine in those waters, and a smile spread across it.

Not a smile of easy contentment or happiness; but a smile of…thrill. For she felt it, starting with a minor sensation, before blossoming and waxing into a glow that spread across her skin and heart. She had finally reached her element, a place where she belonged, and was on the brink of unleashing a new, potent part of herself.

Then she frowned. Something was wrong.

Her reflection didn't smile.

Smash. Like a thunderbolt, a large broadsword shot out of the water, a blade thrust straight at Ira's throat. Snap. She felt her body jerk back as if pulled back by the unseen hands of some giant, tossing her to safety. Then she was nine feet away, watching the blade, taller than her, rise out of the waves, breaking through like a rocket. It was a brilliant silver, unalloyed and lustrous, as if it bore an intrinsic shimmer surpassing the sun's.

But gripping the dark-blue sword hilt was a hand. A dark hand, as if it had been charred and scorched in pits of fire. A bleeding hand, rivers of blood running across its surface, scars gashed into it as if the flesh had been ripped out by toothed whips. Following it was an arm, with muscles ridged on it like a great mountain range, eroded over the millennia, scarred by great astras of the gods that wreaked destruction on its surface, leaving deep indentations of wounds and suffering.

Ira averted her eyes, blanching at the sight of a relic

of banishment to the *Patala*, one of the most hideous punishments the gods ever gave those who sinned. A punishment reserved for who sought to consume worlds in their malice and bloodlust, which ravaged their souls from inside and cast a shadow that shrouded Heaven and Earth, to be dispelled only by the might of a *Deva*, who would consign them to the horrors of hell for eternity, where they would be set ablaze and branded with hot irons and mutilated.

Her vision colored over; her skin paled; and she felt like she would faint.

Then the head came. It was certainly a once handsome face, as the enigmatic black eyes like dark moons and the battle-hardened look with lines of age and war showed. But it too was a patchwork of grisly scars and gashes and pools of blood, that were welling up and cascading down the face, dripping down the chin. A golden crown clung to his head, and it seemed to Ira like it was fixed there, welded into his skull in a forge so that there were areas of charred, black skin around the edges.

The chest too was such, with glorious muscles that bulged and rippled but slashed and defaced by many blades.

The figure towered to thrice Abhay and Ira's height and hefted his enormous blade. Abhay still stood there, looking up at the man in horror.

"I am Mahabali," he announced, his baritone voice

grating through the air and the rocks by the stream. "Conqueror of the Heavens, vanquisher of the Gods. And I have come to wreak vengeance upon Vishnu and his craven, frail, spawn; that God who imprisoned me in the fires of the Underworld!"

Besides him, all along the water, rose several others, shorter than him, but bearing their own swords, each casting shadows of terror across the riverside.

Mahabali's eyes gazed at Abhay like the lidless orbs of a serpent, poised to strike and slaughter his prey. He raised his sword, like an asteroid streaking through the heavens, resplendent in the sun, and brought it down upon Abhay to rend asunder his skull.

But Abhay whipped out, like a blue flash of lightning, his blade, which glowed with an ethereal light like that of Lord Shiva's throat. The runes on its handle blazed, and its surface seemed to simmer with searing hot sparks of divine flame. He brought it up and swung it at the impending weapon, and the two met with a crash like the collision of worlds, sending shockwaves across the land, ripples of might and tremor that felled Ira, and as she lay, sprawling on the ground, the hordes of hell bore down upon her.

Then she closed her eyes. Sometimes, the time was ripe for unleashing her primal beast, her inner vigor and wrath and restlessness. But more often, in the face of darkness and near death, light is found in the most still and tranquil places.

It was not black in her mind; she heard the voice of her mother, like the breath of the heavens, rustling through her being and soothing it, and gently kindling a flame of knowledge, the flame of *maya*, capable of conjuring and razing to the ground all illusions.

She opened her eyes. There were the true beings, not demonic warriors, but mere shriveled-up ghouls of darkness, wretched and pathetic, flapping in the wind like clumps of cloaks, with two emerald-green orbs for eyes. She reached out her hand, and a stream of pink-orange fire pulsed across it like a celestial wave. She pointed her arm and shot out the flame at the creatures, and they were all gone, blown away by the wind of unveiling that thrust aside the curtain on the illusions that they were, figments of some twisted, repugnant, but potent imagination. But she had no time to ponder this, as she looked ahead, and her jaw dropped at what she saw.

***

Abhay gave battle to a demon of hell, primal and seemingly limitless in strength. He felt pain throbbing through his arms and chest when that behemoth of a blade smashed into his, but then came a rush of life force, of divine energy that expelled those feelings of weakness and imbued his soul with new energy. He felt a new flame blaze in his heart, wind gust under his feet, water rush at the back of his throat, and the conch of Vishnu resound above his head. The elements, the forces of creation, the gods, were with him.

Before Mahabali could heft his blade for another blow, he swung his sword back, slicing it through the air and across the broadsword's edge in a blinding flash, sending the demon staggering back. Mahabali shouted in rage and brought his sword in an arc, right for Abhay's neck.

In that hour, staring death in the eye, Abhay remembered something.

He remembered failing to block a punch from his Karate Sensei in the dim darkness of a dojo, long ago, far away. As it thudded into his shoulder, the man, clad in his *gi*, with a red-and-black belt tied around the waist of a white robe, said, "Step away from the line of attack".

That instinct, those words, that muscle memory, all flashed in Abhay's mind in an instant and flowed into his body. He stepped to the left, evading the stroke, while bringing up his weapon in a slash. Blood spurted, and a scar ran across Mahabali's chest. He roared in pain, and his roar was like that of a roaring cosmic waterfall, cascading through eternity and bellowing as it fell into depths of agony and oblivion. Abhay slid away low to avoid any wild, agonized thrashings of the blade.

"Abhay!"

A voice called out, and there were soft but firm arms on his shoulders, as if half-restraining, half-comforting his mind.

He looked to his left and felt that soft, bushy hair, cozen and brush against his face. It was Ira, standing beside him, gazing on at the convulsing Asura with a fey, watchful, glance, as if she was unraveling great secrets in his being.

***

There it was, right before her eyes.

There was no form. Nothing. Absolutely nothing stood before her.

She'd been staring at the demon before her, thrashing in agony from the injury inflicted on him by the divine blade, and he'd seemed all too real. However, when she'd again allowed herself to sink into the depths of consciousness, in the realm where her mother's powers were potent, there was just empty air in front of her.

Abhay had seemed calmed by her coming beside him, but as he allowed his rational, usual instincts to take over, his breath quickened again, eyes widened, and he stared at Ira. "Ira, he'll kill us..."

"No, he won't," said Ira, meeting Abhay's eyes with an irrefutable certainty like that of a sage.

She held his hands for a few moments, and Abhay felt a vibration in his palms, and a current flow through his being like a gushing river of wisdom. It felt like the deluge washed away all confusion, all fears, all thoughts- all *illusions.*

He looked up and saw nothing. He stared. Ira laughed.

"I know, it's hard to believe," said Ira. "But that monster who nearly killed you is just an illusion."

Mahabali was an Asura who fought with Lord Vishnu, but was, upon defeat, not tormented in this ghastly fashion, but crowned King of the Netherworld, as a reward for his care for his people and valor.

These were mere phantoms, illusions conjured up by the mages and maya-masters of Kali Asura.

Her mother spoke those words, but Ira didn't need to relay them. She felt understanding dawn in Abhay's eyes, which were now pure and still, not wild, with pure black depths that emanated comprehension, ringed by a white substance like the crescent moon.

There were no words. They both looked at each other, knowing that they'd had their first true test. Sure, Ira had confronted Jara Asura a few days back, but this was the first time they'd fought as one, as Kalki, battling the wrath and machinations of Kali Asura and his forces.

Both of them took deep breaths and found relief in the sudden calm that settled over them. It had been the most frenetic few minutes of their life- out in the cold, battling primal forces of malice without the help of Parashuram. But they'd triumphed, by looking deep inside themselves and channeling their inner heroes, the true essences of their beings, the magic that infused their roots, the primal powers of Devas and Asuras.

Kalki had been born fifteen years ago on each of their birthdays. Kalki had received their guru three days ago, and their three possessions, yesterday.

But in many ways, it felt like today was the day Kalki was truly born- born as a dispeller of darkness, as a true force of nature to raze down Kali Asura's works of spell and fire and keep alight the flame of light and hope, hope for the resurrection of their loved ones and the continued survival of the world, in the age of Darkness.

Invigorated with this new sense of strength, they sat together on the horse, Abhay now taking his turn at the helm, and rode into the sun, across the open plains, resuming their quest.

***

The next few hours were another blur of green plains and sloshing rivers and badlands of gravel. Ira dimly remembered Shuka telling her they'd go on for around five hundred kilometers, but all notions of distance and time seemed to contort, seemed to streamline in a single, endless expanse of motion; a celestial motion that would be equally fast, equally relentless, on all the worlds of the Universe.

And Kalki blazed on, holding on to each other; not out of desperation or fear of falling off their meteoric steed, but out of newfound strength, newfound confidence in their prowess as children of the Gods, as leaders of the light in this troubled age, as writers of their own destinies and makers of their own triumphs; triumphs they would reach after scaling heights together, merging their powers into an unstoppable force that would blast with a divine wind upon the hideous forms of Kali Asura's minions.

They were like the haze of a spacecraft shooting through space, moving so fast that they heated up with a heavenly warmth, rays of light breaking across and around their faces, almost forming halos and wreathing them in a brilliant aura; a mass of luminescence lighting up the fields and illuminating the path ahead.

Devadatta finally paused near a creek, lively, fresh waters frothing and sloshing. A lengthy, chocolate-brown log lay across it as if basking on a cool bed in the rays of the sun. He knelt down to drink the water, and so did Abhay and Ira. Abhay paused before drinking the water, looking down, troubled, as if dreading the waters to erupt and a blade to be thrust into his face. Ira noticed this and placed her arm on his. "It's safe," she said. She didn't know why she knew this, but then, could she really explain any of her knowledge and powers, beyond her lineage as an Asura and a daughter of Maya?

They drank it and felt the cool of the liquid splash across their faces, which, now that they came to think of it, felt parched; parched by the sun, perspiring after the fire of the battle.

As Ira arose, though, after a powerful gulp and splash, she found that part of the aura of perfection and romanticism that had settled in after their victory had cleared. Sure, it was always good to have a refreshed, ready, mind, but often a cleanup revealed little, stray bits of debris from the past that just stuck in the sand a little extra naggingly.

Maa, she said.

She felt it. An awakening in her mind, the arrival of an otherworldly presence, who cast her consciousness across Ira's like the sun spreading its radiance across the Earth and imbuing its heart with that glow. Sometimes, this distance from her mother pained her, especially when it meant she had to face the travails of the world alone. But there was beauty even in distance, if only in how every time the minds of the two connected, it was like their souls, imbued with all that magic and love, embraced each other.

Yes, Putri?

I...I wanted to ask you something. She faltered, in the face of her mother's loving voice, the voice that had been her sole guiding light through the darkness and towards her destiny. But she still needed to know.

At the river, where the maya-made Asuras came out,

*why did you encourage me to go in? I could have...*she stuttered again. *I mean, they were just illusions,* she told herself. *But surely even illusions, when crafted by skillful minds, can be dangerous.*

Yes, Ira. Illusions are powerful. An illusion was powerful enough to make a fire to warm you and Abhay, to withstand the might of a sibling of Kali Asura. But often, more valuable in this world than conjuring illusions, is unveiling them. Casting aside the veil of deceit to your mind, of treachery to your eyes, of false threat to your life, is essential to survival, in a world where many forces, magical or not, will seek to deceive you. Mind-reading? Looking beyond Abhay's friendly demeanor and seeing his real feelings, unearthing the fragile soul of Jara behind that frightening visage, seeing Mahabali and his Asuras for mere phantoms, shades of the night embellished with a single layer that makes them look real...these are all examples of that.

Then Ira got it. Once more, the truth was so simple. She'd begun to worry; worry about that intuitive sense of belonging she'd felt on the banks, which had sparked fresh worries about her identity as an Asura in her; concern at how her mother had seemingly led her straight into danger, egging her on to drink from the water.

But what all she truly needed to do, *what you should have done, Ira, you dolt,* she told herself, *was to have faith: faith in fate*, maneuvered as it was by the hands of the gods, guided as she was through it by the wisdom of her mother.

It's alright, Ira, said her mother, swaddling her troubled mind in the magical, loving blanket of her care. *Life-and-death situations, or really any that stretch the individual, can make even beautiful people like you forget the love and faith that usually keeps them going; the illusion arises that they're alone, without a guiding light, without comrades, bereft even of the fire that has been burning for them all their lives. That, perhaps, is the ultimate Maya you need to learn to see through and overcome.*

Love you, Maa.

Love you too, Putri.

Then there was silence, that blanket that had smothered her mind, troubling it from the tumults of the world, whisked away as if by a celestial breeze, that, even as it departed, left a fragrance that cozened her nostrils and left a tingle of pleasure all down her airways, nuzzling her mind.

But even as she closed her eyes to savor this sensation and get lost in this ethereal world, she felt a movement; a shift in the astral world, on the plane inhabited by celestial beings. She stiffened.

She and Abhay had been standing there the whole time, drinking, whether it was water from the river or the flowing streams of their thoughts. But not until now had she seen, standing on the log, a tall *sanyasi-*

like figure, lower body garbed in a saffron robe, holding an enormous stringed instrument, a veena, across his chest, with the curved form of a *tilak* on his forehead. But he had long, bushy hair that seemed to skip with joy in the wind; and the sparkle on his fair face, of a glimmering smile and eyes that glinted like small stars but were still, as if carefully surveying the surroundings. These signs seemed to kindle something deep in Ira's soul as she intuitively sensed all she saw as hallmarks of a higher being.

"Narayana, Narayana," he said, Abhay was staring at this new arrival, whose voice emanated the same divine voice of Parashuram, but less mystic and solemn and more amused and perceptive.

"I am Narada. God of wisdom, of music, and of stories."

Ira gasped. Was this the first ever God she'd seen in person? But then she felt something falter. He didn't have the awe, the magical aura, that befitted one of the *Devas*...

She saw Abhay beside her smile; the smile of familiarity, but also the smile of amusement, of one who felt himself alone seeing a joke behind the visage of grave words and appearances. "This is the sage Narada," he whispered, inclining his head as he breathed deviously into Ira's ears. "He is no ordinary god; but the son of Brahma."

"But if he's known as anything, it's as..."

Then the god spoke, his voice still imbued with that liveliness, that extra zest that had been so absent in the past few days. "The Lord Vishnu sends me," he said, "To announce that Parashuram, the sixth avatar of the Lord, will not be resurrected."

There was a thump, as if Abhay's heart thudded with one, final, beat, before going into silence.

"Unless" he added, Abhay still a tableau of shock, "His son atones for sins committed in a past life, something which he may achieve by coming forth and prostrating himself before my feet; for I am the foremost devotee of Him who rules over the Universe."

In that quiet, mountains could almost be heard eroding, tectonic plates sliding, as a heart stunned by deathly tidings moved, straining to wrench free of this ice-cold chokehold and prepare the brain and muscles for action.

"The god of trickery," said Ira. Her voice in that moment was like the sudden shining of sprightly sunlight in the middle of a wrathful storm; so poorly understanding the mood, so out of place, and yet so soothing for the souls of those caught in the tempest.

"What?" asked Narada, and in that moment, Abhay saw that veneer of divinity, of wisdom, of calm, shift, and in its place was the stupefied expression of a self-proclaimed pro, beaten thoroughly by one who'd known the game for three days.

Ira stood straighter, and Abhay saw a fire blaze in

her eyes, face setting into an expression of confidence and knowingness. She wrapped her arm around the stunned Abhay's shoulders, leaning her head on his. "Parashuram is safe," she said, glancing at his recently fallen but now restless eyes, before turning to Narada, as if her words were for him too.

"You l..." Then she stopped. Every bit of her heart hungered for vengeance, smoldering with wrath, was on the verge of accusing this man of trickery, of duplicity, of manipulating the feelings of Abhay by resurrecting the specters of three days ago and letting them howl in and torment his mind; but something in her soul stopped her.

This feeling in her, as if infused into her bones or the core of her being, that she should tread with caution. Then, as if serving as an afterthought and maker of the thought at the same time, her mother spoke.

This is the foremost of all rishis, all sages. He has done penance to Lord Shiva and received great boons, and is now a steadfast follower of Lord Vishnu, who sent him here.

The pronouncement of the names of those divinities, those cosmic beings, those forces that shaped this Universe and controlled fate, silenced Ira, frozen as she contemplated what she'd just heard.

At last, she looked at Narada not with an expression of fear or abhorrence, but of perception, of understanding, tinged with a sense of awe and expectance of a mortal about to hear the words of the Gods.

"Hear me, o great Kalki," he said, inclining his head, and placing his hand on his chest. "I sought only to test you," he said, his eyes keenly darting across the scene even as he tried to look apologetic; Ira couldn't help but roll hers, though she reached out and held Abhay's hand tightly when his face that went stiff with rage calmed at her touch.

"I am Narada. The only one who travels between the three worlds of Svarga, Bhuloka, and Patala. Thus, much reaches my ears. Today, Lord Vishnu has sent me here to tell you this: you must make haste. Three days are up out of the seven that the tablet gives you for your quest, and much is left. You head far south now, and rightly so, but after that, your destination is Mount Kailash, on the other end of Bharat."

As he spoke, it seemed to Ira and Abhay as if the path before them, that had seemed too clear and welcoming, something they'd been ready to soar across on the wings of Devadatta, widened. Suddenly, instead of a path of a couple of days through forests and rivers and hills, there were boundless plains as vast as the Earth, on which even the celestial horse would begin to slack and lay upon the ground in exhaustion, and they'd lose themselves in the immensity.

"How will we..." began Abhay, before Narada raised his palm to calm him.

"The gods have laid out a path before you. The

Lord also sends this message: have faith in fate."

"But you must be quick. Even as we speak," he said, a shadow cast across his vibrant face as he looked back whence he came, "A war is being fought. There are shadows on Mount Kailash, cast by the chariots of the Gods. Bolts of flame and thunder and worse things are wreaking death in a war far from the mortal realm."

Then he turned to them, smiled, and bowed. "The Universe is with you two," he said. "Your every word is heard, every shift in your consciousness felt, every decision studied, as if they are imbued with the essence of the cosmos. Should you fail, not only shall the creation of the Gods crumble, but will be at the mercy of a foe that could plunge this world into everlasting darkness."

He bowed a little, and folded his hands, his unbecomingly grave face waxing again with the glow of a radiant, sparkling, smile. "Narayana, Narayana, scions of Devas and Asuras!"

Then he was gone. There was no puff of dust, no fading. Just a complete disappearance, like a celestial wanderer teleporting between dimensions, leaving no trace save the effect of his heavenly presence, his words settling on the air like waves resting on sand and leaving those lain on it awash with bliss and emptiness of mind.

There was silence. Grass rustled. The river gushed. The wind howled. Then Abhay was on the horse, seated straight, legs wrapped around the body as tight and firmly as a warrior. "Coming?" he asked Ira, reaching out his hand, as the parrot fluttered to him and sat on his shoulder.

Ira took Abhay's hand, and then Kalki was once more blazing across the plains, creating a gust of wind that was felt miles away, as the lotuses of Pampa Sarovar stirred; tufts of fine hair on a tail tingled, tickled by the breeze of youth and life; and a pair of dormant eyes blinked open like two suns being born.

SEVEN

Surya, God of the Sun, having arched across the sky, spilling oceans of infinite radiance across the Earth all day, sank a little, beginning to dip as the plains were bathed in an ocean of deep amber and orange and pink. The skies were a tapestry of heavenly beauty that calmed and tickled the senses, lulling them into a boundless sleep without thought or awareness to disturb it, the spirit losing itself in the flaming heavens.

Ira slumped forward. Her billowing cloud of hair, with all its whorls and rivers, did not shroud her face but flowed like streams of the night along Devadatta's body and Abhay's back, where she'd rested her head. Her face was awash with the glow of evening, infused with a deep, blazing, radiance like the core of the sun, awash with a warmth, with the beauty of bliss, a bliss that stroked her face all over and pressed her eyes shut.

Abhay was taken, overwhelmed; taken by the utter contentment that imbued the landscape, that suffused from Ira's form, beautiful in the sheer happiness with which it plunged into the world of sleep. Even Devadatta had begun to slow to a trot, like a fresh, newborn foal on a joyous stroll across the boundless plains, entering what was to him a *svarga* of a new life.

He noticed that Shuka wasn't seated on his shoulder anymore, but was flying by the horse, beating his wings, the neon green of his plumage set aflame to a new incandescence that kindled the fires of Abhay's heart. He, at least, noted Abhay, seemed to be still in the real, physical world, with that same, beady-eyed, focused glint in his eyes and metronomic beating like the susurrations of a sage's heart. Then those beady bluish-black eyes, like the night sky on a full moon night, turned and stared right at Abhay.

Ah, a staring contest, thought Abhay. He stared back. Then one of the eyes flashed as if someone had set the night sky afire with a shooting star. Abhay's eyes throbbed suddenly with pain as if penetrated by the breaking rays of the sun. He could almost feel them rupturing, tears releasing, or was it blood? He lowered his head quickly, hiding in the darkness, buried in his palms. But even in this emptiness where he had only his mind to contend with, he could see Shuka. The parrot's eyes were there, impassive round orbs like dark-blue moons. Then they stirred, beginning to whirl like a cyclone, before spiraling into a furious rotation like a spiral galaxy. Swirls of white raged against the blue backdrop- or was it the blue itself spinning against the blue backdrop? The eyes were no longer circles but battlegrounds, between the stillness and the fierce tempests of motion that seemed to churn Abhay's mind and vision into meaninglessness.

Then there was true emptiness. *Ah,* thought Abhay, distantly. *Atman, not mind, you fool.*

Yes. There was an answering voice, faraway, yet clear. Fairly normal, like that of an assertive, terse man, but also with a certain sprightliness and high pitch like that of a bird; and with the depth and majesty, each syllable waxing and waning as it came, like a god's voice.

Then the voice was…Narada's?

"Today, Lord Vishnu has sent me here to tell you that the prophecy will go waste unless you make haste."

Haste, haste, haste...Abhay's mind lulled by the sunset and lain into a deep sleep-like state by the voice, began to move. Neurons fired; he could feel their heat as they raced along the pathways of his head, whose surface he could feel blazing all over with a flame. He felt something far deeper inside, far more primal, awake; if his mind right now was like the light from the sun, spreading across the solar system and slowly feeding all its inhabitants the vigor of life, this was the sun itself, with the heat of a star system brewing in its depths.

Hell, this was no sun. Nor was this any other pathetic ball of burnt gas or clump of polluted rock that claimed to be a Lord of the Cosmos. This was something that had been there far before any of them, hallowed in a space beyond space; fermented in the formless, eternal mix of the *Brahman*- the pure consciousness that birthed all the *atman*.

This was his soul.

And his soul, emotionless, intangible, and metaphysical though it was, was angry.

It let it show.

Abhay's eyes thrust awake, like two supernovae, and his slothful form stirred like a leaf shaking in a sudden storm, dancing to a new, pulsing music of life and energy. He sat straight again. *Uthapatti, Devadatta*. His *atman* spoke.

The horse tossed his head back and neighed as forcefully as the bellow of Vishnu's conch, its mane of pure white hair billowing in the wind. Behind him, Abhay felt Ira; not a sleepy, restful form, but an alive, powerful one, that gradually raised itself from the bed of Abhay's back, until all Abhay could feel was a sense of power behind him, as if the daughter of Maya had awoken.

He turned right and saw Shuka there. It seemed to him, as the parrot inclined his head, beating his wings at the same breakneck speed, almost as if the beady-eyed parrot were smiling, as if the perpetually stiff mouth curved a bit as if the eyes glinted with appreciation.

He began to speak, again in that same, telepathic way. "Meet a Deva..."

"And get lost forever in the maya of bliss at meeting him or become him yourself," said Abhay, the words coming out as automatically as thundering did when Devadatta ran, as he was doing now.

There was a gentle prod on his back, a sharp jab of a finger thrust in daughterly indignation that somewhat cleared the ethereal air. Abhay sighed.

"Sorry, Ira."

"You do know Maya is the name of a god too, right?"

Abhay was about to reply with "Not a Deva, an Asura," or something lousily semantic like that, but stopped. What was the point anyway?

Lord Vishnu had sent them a message. A divine wind had been sent to guide them on their course; they'd threatened to squander it like fools by letting it lull them into complacency and tickle them to a blissful sleep. But this was what it'd been sent for, gusting with the breeze and letting their spirits soar with it, raging in a tempest of godly might that would blast their foes and storm across the Earth, all the way to Mount Kailash.

***

Devadatta's hooves clip-clopped on a bed of cragged

rocks; probably brown in this semi-arid woodland but tinged with a surreal shade of blue in the night. The sound of the hooves, like deliberate drumbeats, was rare after he'd flown across miles of grass and stone without sound or a clear sense of motion.

Abhay knew that when the horse slowed down like this, it wasn't because he was tired, for he'd never known exhaustion in his whole life. How old was Devadatta? Was he really just two days old? Or was this horse an older being, a steed of one of the gods?

What he saw next nearly convinced him that he was.

For the horse stared right at the thick clump of trees and bushes and brambles before him, and seemed to look right above it, as if gazing obstinately at the heavens, ignoring this vegetation that to Abhay could only mark a dead end in a search for a lake full of lotuses. Then he reared up on his hind legs, his smooth, level back turning into a steep gorge, as Ira shouted in shock and hung on tight to Abhay. Abhay nearly thought the horse would take to the stars, be summoned to the heavens like Parashuram had by Vishnu. But then he lowered himself, and like a battering ram of pure muscle, smashed through the tree wall, as bushes splayed into ragged clumps and branches were torn asunder.

Then there it was. Shining with a clear, bright, aquamarine and deep purple in the moonlight, an ocean of pure color and stillness.

Then Abhay's eyes adjusted to this sight, and he saw not one mass, but the discs of thousands of lotuses, with a surreal, alien green glow in the night, deep pink flowers like stars blooming from the base. These were lain all over a bed of aquamarine water infused with an ethereal, pure light like that of crystals that stirred the lotuses gently with its ebbs and flows, that gave this little, and yet, so infinitely vast, solar system a shining background.

Shuka spoke. Even he seemed captivated, his eyes wide and even stiller than the lake, like small dark blue planets that reflected the beauty of the lake.

"Pampa Sarovar."

There was silence. They gazed, open-mouthed, at all the lotuses, like angelic beings in themselves, hiding their beauty in this glade, but granting them mere mortals a sight, a glimpse into the magic that imbibed this place.

"Now what?" asked Ira.

There was a stir in the waters, a single wave rippling over the lake like the undulation of a serpent, as small waves slid across it before breaking on the rock at their feet. The breath of the four held in awe suddenly felt to Abhay like bated breath, breath held in trepidation. With one hand, he reached into his pocket and produced the tablet. With the other, he pulled his sword from Devadatta's back and unsheathed it.

The blade felt dead; gone was the sense of celestial

power from earlier in the day. It was pale, pale silver, like a shade of its former self, helpless, pallid in this world of fear and darkness, and a beauty that, suddenly, felt almost ghostly.

Then the water erupted. Its surface was ripped apart, thousands of lotuses falling and raining down on the trees, gigantic waves thrown from the center, crashing into the banks with the force of a tsunami.

And in its place arose a pillar of water, the flowing streams that were the origins of the flayed waves gushing and roaring and gliding over each other, together towering into a whirlpool five times as tall as the trees. It was as if it was funneled up into the heights of the heavens, a raging tumult of aquamarine that blazed with an oceanic brilliant blue fire, unchallenged by the darkness of the night. Then, from the top of the whirlpool, simultaneously a few dozen feet and worlds away, a face looked back.

That of a woman, with empty eyes like pearls of pure white that shined like deathly pale moons against the bright blue, hair billowing in the whorls of hundreds of swirling streams of water. There was also a mouth and a nose, creations of the water, and gargantuan arms and legs that thrust out of the water as if brewing divine energies and forces to manifest them into tremendous physical forms as long as spiral arms of galaxies.

Then it was no longer a cosmic tornado or whirlpool, but a woman, head meeting the sky and feet meeting the water, surrounded on all sides by a single, curved, wall of waves, breaking incessantly on the trees, as if it contained all the waters in the world.

The pale, lidless, vacant eyes fixed themselves on Abhay and Ira, like those of a snake observing its prey.

Then the wave wall shifted, and it was no more circular but an infinitely wide and tall mass, as if all the water in the oceans was rearing up and breaking upon its helpless victims. It bore down upon them, and in it, Abhay saw the fangs, blood-red eyes, and pale broadsword of Bhaya, and the thunder of Kali Asura as it smote his father in tempestuous skies. It was not just the water, but all the tumult of the past few days that crashed upon Abhay, inhuming his soul and the entire land in a tsunami.

Then he blinked. Ira was holding aloft her right, clenched fist, which was blazing with a flame; a still one, yet one that stirred in its blazing depths like the core of a red supergiant star, fiery yet chilly, bringing warmth and yet a comforting cold, so that Abhay felt his soul awash with infinite bliss and calm.

The wall of waves had not yet fallen; it had paused in its deathly descent, a few inches above the fire, and was now colored with that mixture of amber and blood red all over, as if set afire. Ira was also illuminated by the splendor of the flame, her face, her arms, awash with that radiance, her hair wild and raging in many whorls around and across her face.

"Stop this, Danu," she said, and Abhay saw her stand straight as her voice boomed. "I am the daughter of Maya, whose art you seek to use on us." She brandished her flaming right hand and brought it upon the body of the wave in a brutal blow. Then, like a curtain of illusion being parted, blown away by the wind of unveiling, the waters dissipated, falling into nothingness, mingling with the waters of the once more placid lake, bathed all over by moonlight and its pale blue radiance.

But still, levitating at its heart, was a woman, robed in bright blue, hair streaming like the outflow of water from the now-dead tsunami. Her skin was pale, like the moon, and her eyes were blue, much more so than Shuka; for it felt like the entire Earth was held in each of them. After all, no matter how many continents were carved, mountains raised, forests grown, deserts laid, water held sway. Its stronghold was the infinite ocean, but its forces permeated the land, running across it in rivers, cascading in waterfalls, welling up in lakes; and this lake was its home.

"Daughter of Maya?" she asked, her voice dripping abhorrence, imbued with foreboding of calamity like luckless souls slowly being dragged out into the wild tide of the sea. "So, by proclaiming that you are the spawn of one of my kin, you expect me to spare you? To shower you with familial love, with blind faith in you for your blood, with forgiveness for your mother's loathsome treachery?

"You have the power to unveil illusions, and to make them. But do you have the power to end the biggest illusion of all with one blow?"

Then she glanced at the water; but in her glance was not fire, as Abhay would usually have described any powerful gaze, but water, like the crest of a wave and its body like the wall of the night as it bore down to destroy.

Instantly, a stream of the fluid arose, like a dead spirit conjured to abrupt awakening, and blasted upon Ira's chest with immense force, slamming her against a tree, tearing the trunk asunder, like a shipwreck left by the raging deeps, its felled, frail, sailor lain before it.

Time froze. The same forces kicked in Abhay's mind as had twice before when faced with Kali Asura and his minions. It felt as if a deathly-cold blade had gashed his head, which was awash with blood that suffused across his mind, filling its surface with a feral flame of loss, that blazed with horrifying fervor. Was Ira dead? Tears clogged his vision, before thickly, like clots of blood, dribbling down his cheeks. He shut his eyes. Perhaps it was best to let go. To let himself remain, drifting in this void of darkness, safe from the spectral, ashen, light of day. Let the flame lick at the walls of straw that shielded his wild mind, most of which, now that he surveyed it with the bloodshot eyes of those weary of tumults, was a wasteland of grief. Let the flame raze the walls and blaze for a while in the frigid desert, before fading into a bitter gravestone of frost, lost in the endless hellscape of sorrow.

But even as it burned his mind and began to char his soul, it stopped.

Now, it was just the backdrop, the feeling that saturated the darkness of his mind. He felt it grow more and more distant, as his vision morphed from complete blackness into opalescence, snatches of color splattering the dark. Then it was all a midnight-blue, then a shining opal blue, then a picture of sheer lucidity and beauty.

It was first the blue of the grove of trees on the banks, a deep, dark, navy blue, like waters that had slept, sinking into the bed of sleep; then the blue of the skies above, a midnight-blue, as if the firmament was not a boundless region of emptiness, but a still, watery, ocean; then the aqua-blue of the waters, forming a resplendent, pure, bed of crystal. Then, he saw the brilliant blue of the regalia of Danu, as if sapphires were gilded upon her pallid, fair skin; then the blue of the eyes of Shuka, pulsating and waxing with all the shades of the color, amalgamated into a single, distilled, color that glittered with brilliance and absorbed with the power of the full moon night.

But whatever shade it was, the color emanated a potent vibration, a surging energy that issued from the depths of Shuka's soul, from his *atman*; from the depths of the ethereal expanse of the *brahman*. It was inundated with the essence of being, the divine consciousness that all life, all creations of the Lord, shared.

Abhay heard himself muttering three words.

Om Namah Shivaaya.

Then there was another blue; on the blade that Abhay's hands gripped, aflame with a firestorm of the deepest, most fundamental, blue in existence, that ignited the metal, until it was crackling all over and discharging heat and power like a pulsar.

Then the flame spiraled and poured and rolled into a billowing cloud, snaking through the air in all its magnificence. A cloud of pure divine energy and magic, a deep, spellbinding form that outlined itself against the light-blue lake like the full moon against the darkness of the night.

The runes scored on the blade's handle shimmered with the same cosmic blue, running through the indentations in the metal-like rivers of celestial flame that Abhay's arm illuminated all over with that same color. As if magic was suffusing into his skin and pulsing through his veins. These letters, these syllables of power, and the hilt, glinting with unalloyed heavenly silver, sunk into the palm of his right hand, as if embracing its brother, its kin-spirit, its soulmate. He didn't hold it, grip it like a warrior would a sword; he merely poured all of his love, all of his fire, into returning that embrace, and felt a charge like a thousand lightning bolts pulsate and frizzle through his body, permeating it with an intoxicating sense of power, but also bathing it in pure consciousness. He felt awash with an otherworldly calm, a stolid self-assurance, a sharp blade sheathed by the sheathe of limitless world-destroying potential.

For Abhay, now, there were no thoughts; no emotions; no sights; no sounds. Just action, distant but also so fundamental to his soul, as if what he did next was something he'd known he was capable of all along.

He thrust out the blade. The billowing blue cloud whirled and streamed out, before branching into two arms. One bolted at Danu and crashed into her like a colliding galaxy; the other rushed at and wreathed Devadatta in a shroud like a cloud of illusion.

Then, like nebulas parting to reveal their stellar creations, they receded, dissipating, the blue masses dissipating gently, as if parted by some invisible force of will, to unveil what they had wrought.

There was a ragged, ashen-faced lady in the middle of the lake. It was as if a layer of frost and ashes had been applied on her, coating her robes in a ghostly-grey, and producing flaky, pasty skin like a corpse's. She lay there like one, hunched back as if battered by the elements, one knee raised as she held a few strands of her straw-like hair and gazed upon them with vacant eyes. But there was still a sense of magic, a sense of power, a sense of illusion about her; for she did not fall and sink into the water, or fade into nothingness, but seemed to be suspended in the air. There was a flash, as her bleached eyes flared with sudden shafts of bright blue, like the surface of the sunlit ocean.

Then the other shroud was parted; not slowly coming apart, but thrust into, blasted into disheveled wisps and shreds by an explosion of golden light like a supernova.

A figure blasted through where Devadatta had been. There was a great crown, tall and sharp like a sword-blade, gilded with gold and brilliant jewels like multi-colored space dust, above the face of an eagle; the jet-black eyes like the cosmic dark pulsated in the moonlight, waxing like dark moons. There was a *tilaka* on his forehead, a blood-red stroke, as if a brush had been dipped into the deepest core of his heart and swept across his skin. There was a keen golden beak, curving out like a yellow moon; and branching out from it all, piloting the entire frame and speeding it on through the air, were monumental wings, works of emerald green and maroon feathers, woven together into formidable masses that beat with power. The creature's dark eyes narrowed and glowered straight on at the fallen form of the *Asura*, who gazed up fearfully for an instant before her eyes waxed with a deep purple blue and narrowed, and her body blazed all over with a midnight-blue flame.

As the eagle-man hurtled forth, the beak struck Danu, like the blade of a knife flashing, gashing. A spark glinted as it made contact, sprouting into a firestorm that Abhay could hear charring and incinerating flaky skin, enveloping the two beings in a shroud of flame that rolled and swelled, tendrils flourishing and crackling.

When the flame subsided, there was only the ashen, withered form of Danu, as it had been earlier. For a heartbeat, it was there in the air, before falling into the water with a plop. Water rippled from the center, spreading out in wavelets that flowed outwards across the lake. The center-spot marked the grave of Danu, the Primordial Queen of Waters; a grave lain by Lord Garuda, the winged heavenly mount of Lord Vishnu, who had manifested as a thundering steed for Abhay and then revealed his true self to smite Danu.

As Abhay gazed at the placid waters, not a trace; no snatch of cosmic light, no drop of blood, no torn garment, no fallen tree, was left from the fierce battle of gods.

He was wordless as he looked down at the lake. His sword had…Devadatta had…he shook his head as if to clear it of the daze. He glanced down at himself, unharmed, and then panic arose in his giddy mind, like a piercing shaft of flame, burning along his spine and starting a blaze of panic that raged within.

He got up and crashed through the trees, the air misty through the haze of terror and the thick tears. There she was- Ira. Her sprawled form, with her disheveled hair strewn like storm clouds and the ragged turquoise top she'd worn all this time, gleaming in the night. Her face was devoid of the life, the vigor, the fire that made her who she was.

He sank down on his knees. The heavenly power, the bliss that had burned through him and enabled him to strike Danu, sank into the void of loss, and was nowhere to be found now. He had no power that could revive and save his companion. It had been just a few days ago when he had bristled at the sight of Ira in the school corridor, but that felt like an eon ago.

How could he go on without her?

What would he do now?

In his grief-addled state, it took him a while to realize that he was not alone. Someone was standing over him.

Then he looked up into the face of none other than Lord Hanuman.

He was tall, towering far above Abhay, at least eight feet in height. His skin pulsated and radiated a pure golden, full of life and energy. His eyes were like evening suns, deep red, like oceans of love. The smile on his face was like the smile of the sun's rays splashing across the morning sky. His plump cheeks were red-pink, like the calm, warm tones of the sunset clouds. There was a crown on his head; simple, seated there humbly and without much ornamentation, but glittering with radiance, a declaration of its wearer's power, as if the symbol of the might at the heart of all this beauty and benevolence. For his arms and chest were ridged with muscles like canyons had been carved into them, pulsing with power and, he thought, shining with the brilliance of lightning. He wore a golden belt and an ocean-blue loincloth that flapped in the wind, with more lustrous bracelets and bands adorning his arms. There was a thin, black thread around his neck; unassuming and plain to the unaware eye, but Abhay saw in its fabric deeply set power and force, as if it represented some greater being, like a relic of the heavens. Behind him, as if summoned by his divine presence, the sun rose above the horizon, and the landscape was awash with the amber glow of dawn.

Tears streamed down Abhay's cheeks; but these were not the misty tears of grief, but the clear, flowing ones of joy and love.

He bowed deep and folded his hands, as they shuddered with the sheer force of devotion with which they were clasped and the outpouring of hope as he beheld the Chiranjeevi before him. The one who had set Lanka afire, whose bones were infused with the very *vajra-astra* the heavens were now warring over.

"Lord Hanuman!" Part of his mind thought he should say praises and prayers now, but his mind pushed on through that, toward the only goal he could now think of. "I beg of you with my life...will you save my companion, Ira?"

Then something happened that stilled his breath and stemmed his tears; muscular arms reached out and gently lifted Abhay, so that he stood straight, facing Lord Hanuman.

It felt like a lifetime of bliss, of Abhay's mind taken to new heights, from the worries of mortals to a stillness of the divine realm, where he somehow only found calm, a sense of inevitability deep in his soul. Lord Hanuman spoke.

"Jai Shri Ram."

The words were not uttered but were whispered by the soul, poured forth both like dripping water from a wet leaf and rain issuing from the heavens, cooling Abhay's heart and awakening and kindling something in his soul.

Abhay was suddenly awash with hope, with love, with joy; but he also felt small. He knew he was in the presence of a being infinitely greater than him, with an age and powers incomprehensible to his mind. Then Lord Hanuman spoke, and his voice was like the blowing of Lord Vishnu's conch, like the emanating of the five syllables of *Namah Shivaaya*, for it was filled with divinity and limitless power, but also compassion and bliss.

"I will save her; it is my *Dharma.*" he said.

Then he thrust out his fist at the sky and was in the air, soaring onward, arms by his side, smooth as an eagle, gliding into the Sun at superhuman speed.

Abhay watched him depart with awe, and felt his heart warm a bit, hope welling up like the balm for his troubled spirits, as he gazed upon Ira's fallen figure. He reached out and stroked her cheek, and some of her hair, which he'd gotten so used to seeing billowing wildly in the wind. "You'll be safe," he said, softly; and he knew, somewhere deep inside, that this was true.

In a short while, a shadow loomed on the ground, and he felt the movement of a great being through the air near him, wind gusting and billowing around the push of a powerful form. Then there he was, before Abhay's expectant eyes, the Lord Hanuman.

He opened his right palm and Abhay saw in it a single herb, light green, in the shape of a small snowflake, resting on his hand, wreathed by the golden radiance of sunrise.

He nodded to Abhay, as if to signal that deliverance from this pain had come; those orange eyes, like setting suns, blinked and gazed into the depths of his soul as it to soothe it and calm it down. Abhay felt something rest in him; he felt his wild mind settle in the folds of that little leaf, rustle with hope and awakening as the leaf stirred in the morning breeze. Lord Hanuman touched the leaf softly against Ira's arm, brushing a blood-red gash, and then shimmering with an ethereal light, leaving healthy, smooth skin, shining in the morning sun, when lifted.

Distantly, he thought he heard the voice of Lord Hanuman call to him; bidding him to move away so the healing may be done in privacy. Part of him hesitated to leave Ira, so vulnerable, so grievously wounded, alone; but then another part of him welled up and enveloped his mind in an aura of calm and reassurance, and love for the one who guarded and was curing her of her ailment. He entered the grove and sat on a moss-coated rock, overlooking the placid waters of the lake. Gone was the spectral, heavenly aquamarine, brilliant in the night; but this was beautiful, in a different way.

It was placid, as before, but seemed to be sparkling with joy, with life, with serenity, in the morning sun, shimmering on its tranquil surface. Somehow, the lotuses, flung aside by Danu, had come back; not deep purple, but vibrant pink, blooming all over, casting their whorls in a display of flowering, of growth, of the little spark of life blazing away and flourishing. He felt his heart blaze away and bloom as he beheld this; it all seemed to sink in now that he could feel, in his soul, as if the Lord Hanuman's eyes were gazing into it, a sense of stillness. What he'd done with the sword, power surging forth unlike any he'd ever witnessed, the power of the Lord Shiva, wielded by his hands. But he felt no pride, no childish excitement, no disbelief, just simple belief. Faith. Not just in the powers and greatness of the Gods and in fate, but in himself. He was where he belonged; the first time he'd ever known this on a bewildering and tumultuous journey. Sure, there had been moments of triumph, such as the prayer at Trimbakeshwar, the victory with Ira over Mahabali and his troops, and the moment of realization when he awoke everyone from their stupor last morning. There had been moments of warmth, when sitting by the fire with his father, with Ira. But there had been no moments with such sheer realization, of what he was capable of, of what he could do, of who he truly was.

As he sat thus, there was the sound of bushes being parted. He turned to his right, and Ira sat by his side; in perfect health, her wild hair gusting in the wind, her face radiant with that same, spirited, joyous look, as her eyes widened when she took in the beauty of the lotuses. Soundlessly, she shifted over and hugged Abhay, and Abhay felt thick tears stream down his t-shirt. He wiped her tears with his fingers, and without any words being exchanged, just by touch, just by the soft rustle of their breath, just by their thoughts, flowing on another plane as their souls made contact, they knew just how inseparable they had become.

As they came apart, Lord Hanuman stood there, smiling, and Abhay could see a glow spreading across his face and chest. A glow of contentment, with peace, with love for those he'd been sent to protect, as he saw them finding solace and warmth in their companionship and the work of his healing.

Then his massive form stooped a bit, until he was in a plank-like position, his whole back before them. "Climb on," he said. Abhay's heart skipped a beat; he could feel Ira's face still and her eyes shone with wonder as she processed those words.

Abhay and Ira turned and saw Shuka, with those same beady eyes. They still blazed a celestial midnight blue, but seemed to have calmed, like a tempestuous sea stilling to a tranquil resplendence. It seemed like even the parrot had found peace. He did not do as he usually did- look into the distance, fix them with those eyes, or speak in their minds.

He merely looked right at them, that piercing gaze even sharper and more pointed than before and spoke.

"Farewell, Kalki." His voice boomed out, as if in his words was the might and depth of the heavens, as if some gods were speaking through him.

They knelt by him and caressed the bird, allowing him to rest his head on their knees. For the first time, he closed his eyes and seemed in true peace.

"Shuka", said Ira. "Since you know all, I had one last question. Will we emerge victorious?"

Then those eyes opened, and they were like electric blue spiral galaxies, whirring around, as if deep in fervent thought. They felt sucked into them as if they were the whirlpools of time and fate that would inevitably find them and were immersing them day by day in the machinations and magic of the gods.

At last, he spoke. "Have faith in fate, faith in your faith, and faith in yourself."

Then the eyes turned black.

"Till we meet again, Lord."

Then he was gone, leaving no sign of his presence.

They climbed on, Abhay clinging onto his shoulders, trying to wrap Lord Hanuman's bulky, muscular form in an embrace, to show perhaps with a hug his gratitude and love for the monkey-god. He felt Ira climb on behind him and hold on to him.

Then Lord Hanuman took to the skies, blasting through the crowns of the trees, through the gusting wind currents, and they were taken by the might of Lord Hanuman into the firmament and the golden sky. They soared onward into the dawn of their dreams, onward on the celestial path where they both knew in their souls awaited deliverance- of them, of the world, of their loved ones.

EIGHT

The off-brown, boundless neon-green plains, thick forests, light-brown arid woodlands, and serpentine rivers spread out in a limitless panorama below Abhay and Ira. There were the occasional cities, and they felt clumsy, works of concrete and asphalt fixed into the landscape with amateurish artifice and skill. There were the drab forms of buildings, the dark channels of roads, of highways cutting across the plains. Abhay and Ira had lived in one of the world's biggest cities and had gotten so lost in its interiors that it had felt like their whole world. Yet, from this view, they felt lost; lost in the vastness of nature, in the creations of the gods that had been growing and rustling and flowing for eternity. Lost in the immensity of the Universe, in which they were but a speck of dust, governed by the wills of beings with an existence impossible to comprehend, Lost and forgotten in the current upheavals of the world, which lay on a knife's edge, on the edge of a precipice that humanity was oblivious to.

Indeed, up here, the vistas of the Earth, after a few minutes, felt limiting. True beauty was in the gusting wind, in the rushing clouds, in the flight of Lord Hanuman, in the endless azure firmament, in each other's thrill at soaring through the heavens. Even Abhay surprised himself by feeling not just admiration and bliss at the experience, but a thrill. His spirit raged in the billowing gusts of wind, with Ira's dancing hair, and reveled in the power that he felt pulsate within him; the power of the Lord Vishnu's conch, of Lord Shiva's *trishul*, of the divinity pulsing across his body, emanated from Lord Hanuman's back; but also, the power of freedom, of flying. Of being unconstrained, liberated from the limits and worries of his life as a human, and the power of the companionship of a kindred spirit who would be free and wild with him.

"So, Lord," said Abhay, voice imbued with the vigor of life, seeming to echo in the sky and resonate back from the mountains that ridged the plains below. "How did you come to save us?"

There was a pause. Then the voice came, and Abhay found himself awash with joy, with love, with bliss and peace as he heard Lord Hanuman speak again. It was unlike any voice he'd ever heard, different even from Parashuram's. For while he'd, awestruck, often recalled its depth, its majesty, its texture, as if every syllable were rubbed with a spark of divine magic, he didn't have any such words to describe Lord Hanuman's. It just was. It felt like Abhay was looking into the core of the pure consciousness, the *Brahman*, that transcended the Universe, where every being's *atman* resided. It had no easily describable character, no common human emotion that it made Abhay feel.

"Near Pampa Sarovar was a *mandir* devoted to me, on a hill. The mandirs are our homes, in a sense, for each of them houses part of our being. I knew you were coming from before, for all fate is pre-ordained. I sensed your impending arrival in my being, and that it was part of some great plan, some great quest, which would determine the fate of the world. But only when the waters of the *Sarovar* stirred, and the destructive power, the *maya* and maya-unmasking of Lord Shiva flowed through the lake, did I feel the call to come, as if summoned by a divine presence, much like the call of my beloved master, Shri Ram."

Ira's eyes lit up, as if with sudden realization, and she held her hand to her mouth, as if in simultaneous shock and shame.

"What is it?"

"The one with lightning in arms, feet, and tail..." she said, lifting her hand and then staring into space as if her thoughts were racing to catch up with the forces of time and confusion, pondering something that was so lucid and simple yet had been veiled by her engrossment with the events of the past few days.

Lord Hanuman's head turned and a knowing grin flashed across his face, sparkling not with bliss or beauty but mischievousness and knowing. "That's me," he said, before Ira could stutter any more.

"Bajrangbali," said Abhay, and he could see Lord Hanuman start, as people do when their name is called without warning, and not as expected. "That's what that name means, doesn't it? *Bajrang* is thunder and *bali* is lightning."

He reached into his pocket for the tablet and recoiled in an intuitive horror when his hands groped at an empty interior of fabric. "Where…?" his breath and face congealed, as a shiver rustled down his spine. There was a laugh; deep and imbued with a unique, heavenly quality, but also tinged with humor, with amusement, that warmed Abhay's heart.

"It's here," Lord Hanuman said, passing it up to Abhay with his right palm, who gripped it like one holding a long-lost loved one. "I was reading it, and I see myself mentioned." he said. "But as *lightning in legs, arms, and feet.*"

"Shouldn't it be 'the mighty, flying, monkey-god or something…?" asked Ira, gaze frozen in consternation. Then she caught what she'd said, and her eyes widened, appalled, and her half-formed reply stuttered and spluttered its way into silence. There didn't seem anything wrong with that line in itself, but when in the presence of, indeed on the back of a god, it felt trivializing, at worst insulting to such a great being.

Hanuman laughed again. "No, it's alright; if what you said is wrong, calling you an Asura is too. It should be *an avatar of the Lord Vishnu, savior of worlds, daughter of Maya and Pralaya.*"

"Besides," said Abhay, surprising himself, but feeling at ease on the shoulders of this figure of legend and myth, "What could be insulting about monkeys? They are great beings; an army of them fought beside Lord Ram, and the Hanuman Langurs saved Lord Hanuman's life when his tail was set on fire in Lanka before he flew free and razed the city to the ground."

Ira's eyebrows raised, before she looked down, her slowly stirring thoughts shimmering on her face as if she was looking at the topic of discussion like she never had.

Abhay laughed at her expression and turned to look at Lord Hanuman again, but found his joyous mind stilled, quietened, swimming in an ocean of bliss and devotion, when he saw Hanuman's hands folded, eyes closed, lips stirring as they breathed into the air. He emanated a soft vibration that fluttered from his soul and spread through the sky, touching something deep in Abhay's being.

"Jai Shri Ram." Then he turned and smiled at

Abhay; a smile kindled by an unspoken yet so clearly understood and limitless love, which was flowing through Lord Hanuman's heart.

Then the moment passed. but was not blown away with the wind of time like most others, but drifted on it, embracing it with a beautiful fragrance, before the wind blew on.

"Well, yes, before I had lightning or even knew the word, I was just a young monkey, gazing out at the sun. Its deep orange glow radiated beauty into my heart like a ready-to-eat mango. I soared up, only for Lord Indra to strike me down. My father, Lord Vayu, the God of the Wind, sucked out all air from the Universe. The lord of lightning was forced to heal me and bestow upon my limbs the power of *vajra*."

"It feels weird to call you 'lightning' in the prophecy," said Ira. "I mean, that's like calling me illusion; *maya*, which happens to be my mother's name!"

The lord chuckled, before nodding, eyes surveying the sky as if his mind studied some truth unseen to Abhay and Ira. "You're right, Ira," he said, voice distant. "We're not defined by our powers. Yes, you can conjure and unveil mystifying illusions, and Abhay with his might inherited from his father, can vanquish primordial forces of malice, but you two are more than just carriers of magical energies due to lineage; you are...you. Kalki is a warrior for justice, raising a banner against the void of Kali Asura and a future plunged in chaos and darkness, bereft of the control and worship of the *Devas*. You two are Kalki, and your identity as this hero, this avatar of Lord Vishnu, is a product of your strengths, of your personalities. Ira, naturally infused with the wildness, the restlessness, the tempestuous power of your kin. Abhay, mind dancing with the shadows of gods and prophecies, filled with a mysterious yearning for the past, for the tales of old, for fantastical landscapes and adventures."

Abhay and Ira were silent. They looked inside and saw themselves as they never had. They were not just the ancient souls, the *atman* at their core, they'd discussed by the fireside some days back; nor were they just the wild, tempestuous storms of their minds. They were a fusion of both, forged together in divine fires of fate and creation.

"Powers mean nothing without a worthy wielder to harness them for good," Hanuman continued, a darkness suddenly casting itself across his bright face, as he gazed on feyly into the horizon. "The very *vajra* that gave me strength, in the hands of the evil ones, threatens to desecrate our mandirs and cast an eternal shadow on our world."

There was silence, but not a void; not an empty one of fear and foreboding, as had been too many of the past few days. It was one of shared feeling, of intimacy, of unity for a common cause, of the dawning of a new understanding of self. Abhay and Ira's eyes met, and it seemed like they gazed not at each other's faces, or what they thought they perceived of each other's minds, but into each other's souls, imbued with a new sense of clarity, of purpose. Whatever happened, they would join forces, braving all the dangers that Kali Asura placed in their path; for they both knew that the day so far, though long and at times arduous and terrifying, had been day. Now awaited a final nightfall, a night of blood and specters and wizardry and goodness knows what else, upon the dark, frigid slopes of Mount Kailash, godly and mighty, but in another world. In a space and time that transcended anything they'd yet seen. And they needed to be ready.

Abhay saw the fire blazing in Ira's eyes; but this was not wild in a stray way, like that of an outlaw tearing across the world, but of a warrior. Of one prepared to unleash their inner madness with a knowledge that it would emerge victorious, razing to ashes the forces of darkness. Ira saw the silent confidence and assurance, on Abhay's stolid face, the black depths of his pupils pulsing and reflecting sunlight like the ancient ones of Parushram had that night in the forest.

This moment too passed; and then they were gazing onward, over Hanuman's shoulders at the infinite world before them.

As they looked at the landscape at their feet, though, they noticed something beyond a monotonous vista of green and gray, of forest and plain and city.

They noticed, as if glowing like the full moon against the darkest night sky, small in size but infused with a special brilliance, towers of scaffolding and the erected frames and pillars of light-brown brick, the little, snaking shapes of cranes and digger trucks wielding and carting materials.

Lord Hanuman once more clasped his hands in prayer to his master, whom he kept in the depths of his heart, and revered and loved for posterity.

"This is Ayodhya," he said. "The temple of Shri Ram is being constructed at his birthplace; a fitting monument to the devotion of humankind to the Lord."

Something came over Abhay and Ira as they beheld the sight and heard Hanuman's loving words; for though little could be seen of the soon-to-come temple, they felt as if it emanated special energies, fundamental to their being, to some sacred truth; fundamental to, realized Ira, remembering the banyan tree and her mother, her roots.

"You have lived a very long life, Lord," said Abhay, his voice expansive and yet profound, as if reverberating through the stone of the mandir and reflecting not the words of a 15-year-old, but of a soul gazing upon the, by mortal's standards, virtually eternal lifespan of a great being.

"Yes," he said. Then his orange eyes, which Abhay saw lightening, as if tinged with the mellow hue of nostalgia, of ancient love, of fond memories, glimmering as his gaze wandered across the plains below. "I lived in Ayodhya for a short while after Lord Ram returned victorious from the war in Lanka. I kept visiting here in the guise of a *brahmana*, offering puja to the Lord every day. This went on into the next *yuga*, for I never tired of doing penance to the one whom I loved and was devoted to for eternity. Then, Lord Ram manifested into a new avatar of the Lord Vishnu, Lord Krishna. I longed to see him, but when Narada *muni* asked me if I would like to, I said I would await the summons or presence of the Lord himself, for that would mean he wanted to meet me. Then one day, as I served *prasad* to the devotees, I saw the feet of my Lord; it was Lord Krishna! I was overjoyed and filled with a happiness greater than any I'd ever felt, save when I served Lord Ram."

He turned to Abhay and Ira, and saw still faces, taking in all that was being revealed to them.

"Every avatar of the Lord Vishnu is a manifestation of the Lord Ram; whether in the *yuga* of peace or the *yuga* of darkness, whether in the body of a young boy or a formidable warrior. I am devoted to them all, to serving them, loving them, and saving them when they are in need of me. That is why," he said, meeting Ira's eyes now, which were empty but yet shimmering in those depths with an awakening to new wisdom, "My physical body appeared immediately, all the way from my *samadhi*, my deep meditation in the Himalayas, to my *grha*, the house of my *atman* in the temple near

Pampa Sarovar, when through the energies of that temple I sensed you in distress, and the power of Shiva, wielded by Abhay."

They soared over landscapes, slowly with time becoming less green and more white and gray, the ancient, stone-welded, forms of mountains, coated with thick snow caps.

"These are the Himalayas. The sacred mountains in the north of this country, surpassing any that will ever be made in their stature and power." Then something happened that pulsed in the depths of Abhay's soul, stirring the core of his being and opening some part of it to a new revelation, offering a glimpse of a higher truth. His face fluoresced with a sudden deep blue, like the background of the boundless cosmos, like the blue flames running along Abhay's sword last night; then the color settled, as if changing from a blaze to a hue that permeated the face and left it blue all over. The face seemed now to reflect not just the beauty and love of Lord Hanuman, but a sense of stillness, of infinite wisdom and eminence. The orange eyes were no more like sunsets but like entire universes in themselves, bathed in the flame of a deep, holy radiance that created and illuminated and immolated. The voice that spoke next was Lord Hanuman's, but yet was as if spoken not from the mouth before Abhay, but from everywhere in the Universe, issuing like the words of one who transcended space and time and yet was everywhere, for all was but the work of his will, of his power, of his *samadhi*, of his illusion and his love and his…being.

"Devi Shakti manifested herself as the daughter of these mountains, as the beautiful Parvati, to be as wife to Lord Shiva. To be by his side and sit with him on a high seat in the mountains, in a *svarga* of peace and bliss. Who could stir even the most pure and steadfast *yogi* Shiva with attachment and undying love."

"Where are they now?" asked Abhay. He didn't know why; the answer seemed obvious, but he felt lost in another world when he heard the voice. When he heard holy words of the greatest of deities and their existence, he yearned to be there forever. Not with some base desire, but with the purity of the soul wanting to be safe in its home.

"On Mount Kailash," he said, and Abhay's existence was filled with a rapturous and yet pure, tranquil, bliss, as he saw the face wax, the radiance of the full moon cast across it for an instant, the shadows of mountains and the eternal night framed upon it, before merging into it, suffusing into the blue-tinged face and leaving an indescribable color. Abhay discerned a formless beauty; a still energy that pervaded his soul and being, and the entire Universe was the infinite beauty of that truth.

He looked at the horizon and saw the last vestiges of the sun disappear over the horizon.

"It will soon be night," said the voice, and this time

there was no mistaking. It was deep with knowing, with the kind of immortal knowledge and consciousness that flourished in the profundity of thoughtlessness, with the understanding of one who was seeing what was happening, already perceiving the future, already perceiving the past, already present everywhere, in all times and in infinite spaces.

"The full moon will illuminate the dark waters of Lake Mansarovar, and Shiva and Parvati will bathe in it, as is their custom, their infinite souls and beings awash with the waters of that holy lake. Around them will be arrayed the glimmering lights of the *vimanas* of the gods."

Then the voice changed one last time. Rather, it was the same, just as pure, just as divine, but to Abhay's mind seeming more authoritative, more clearly someone other than Lord Hanuman.

"And I will be there, with the crescent in my matted hair and the *rudraksha* beads around my blue-pulsating neck, holding my trishul, awaiting the arrival of the tenth avatar of Vishnu, of the two called Kalki, to speak to them and bless them as they wait on the final night before the final battle."

Then it passed but did not quite; it seemed merely to settle on the breeze, on the wind, as if not blown away or lost but permeating it, spreading its consciousness, its supreme self across the Universe, and imbuing everything with a peace and lucidity it had had all along but not known it, caught in the flurry of their minds and the tempests of their worldly existences.

Abhay looked at Lord Hanuman's face and saw that the glow that had filled his soul with awakening, with purity, with peace, was gone; and yet was there at the same time. There was the lord, in all his radiance and beauty and bliss, cheeks shining deep red and deep orange eyes like mangoes, with golden life-infused skin; but there was also…there was also…there was also…he couldn't say it.

Then he was back in the physical world. He was now not in some faraway world, beyond everything, where notions of time and space were irrelevant; he was in the Himalayas. A frigid breeze thickened by snow blew by and froze Abhay's skin; Hanuman flew through dark mountains coated by white snow, casting their ancient shadows on them, towering high into the sky.

Then they flew straight into a snowstorm; a void of snow falling and a cold breeze gusting at their chattering teeth and shivering skin. There was nothing to be seen, heard, or felt, for even the sensation of the cold passed, seeming to sink into their skin and settle into their being as if this was another world full of bliss and peace.

Then at last Lord Hanuman thrust through the mist; and before them, arrayed on an endless plain of rock and acres of snow, were two vast lakes. One, to their right, stood still, nestled in the cavity hallowed for it, waters unmoving, shimmering with a special beauty, like a vast vat of undiluted consciousness. "Lake Mansarovar," Abhay whispered, his voice husky and faint and yet echoing in the cold winter air. Behind him, he felt Ira tense, and a strong and warm grip around his back, with the apprehensiveness of astray souls about to be cast out into the world of belonging, where they'd been at home, in peace, all along. He remembered, somehow, as if it were not so long ago and yet in a distant lifetime, watching reels next to Vihaan in the bus, images of the formidable Mount Kailash, of the blustery waters of Rakshastal and the placid ones of Lake Mansarovar playing out on the phone screen. They had just been distant curiosities then, at best imbued with what his mind perceived as a mystic, arcane quality.

As Ira glanced to her left, she beheld another lake. She'd been awed by the beauty of the other one, but as she looked at this one, its waters conjured something in her soul. No, kindled it, for this was no art of *maya*, but something that stoked the fires deep in her being and made her wish to dance with the thrashing dark blue waves that broke upon each other and the banks in a chaotic frenzy of primal energy. She closed her eyes as they transported her across time and space, to the night her father had died, when the rolling thunder and cascading rain by the dark Juhu Beach had taken her soul on an odyssey. On a journey that began with primal impulse, with wanderlust, with an urge to follow her call and the love of one who called herself her mother. She felt a tear roll down her cheek, and then she felt an embrace; an embrace like the embrace of the heavens, of a mortal mind bathed in starlight and clouds, yet far deeper in essence. For this was the embrace of a mother and embrace that told her that through all that journeying, that wandering, she'd found herself, her roots, her home.

He will come back, Ira; and you know it. Let your restless soul soar; this is where you belong.

Love you, Maa. Love you with all my life and soul.

She turned, smiling, feeling her spirit truly free; for while the fight for freedom was filled with rage, with belligerence, with valor, true freedom had only... calm; purity; and an endless joy, not the kind of fleeting euphoria the crashing thunder had brought to her air-conditioned, socially conditioned, drab life.

Then she heard it; for the first time in what felt like eons: her inner voice speaking to her.

Oh, come on, Ira. Have some fun!

Then she let it course and blast through her; the crashing, writhing waves far below, the wailing winds, the frosty mountain-cold, flowing along her shivering spine and skin. Her raging heart stirred and cried out in a primordial delight, as she screamed, raising her hands aloft, her voice booming back from the mountains and amplifying it like the call of the wild itself, a call she'd heeded and now was making, as if her heart was saying: I am here. I am where I belong, where I thrive, where I rule.

She turned to look straight ahead, and as she saw it, the scream went away, as if finding the rest of its bellowing, joyous crescendo, in the mountain that stood before her.

It raised its head out of a mass of smaller, grey hills that rolled about its feet. It was not the unforgiving spire, the cold work of stone she'd come to think mountains were. It was curved, as if welded not from harsh stone, but from the flowing waves of the ocean of the cosmos, churning out the purest form of existence and merging with each other in a rounded shape that was like the entirety of the Universe, everything in it fused together and mixed into a shape that contained it all.

It was like a pyramid, bent or molded into a still roughly pyramid-like shape that was quite unlike anything she'd ever seen.

Next to her, Abhay gazed on at it with the same wonder. "That lake…" said Ira, "was unlike anything I'd ever seen…"

Abhay looked into Ira's eyes, so wonderstruck, so distant, and yet infused with a beauty of realization and of peace mixed with that wildness. He felt as if he knew her, as if he knew what she was feeling, and thinking, her soul quietened and yet wild at the sense of pure belonging when she looked at the lake. He smiled.

"Yes, the shiny one, right? The still one. So holy… Shiva and Parvati will bathe in it at night."

"No," she said, and her eyes flashed with a flare of irritation at her bliss being interrupted by someone who had no understanding of what she was going through. "The other one: the wild, restless, free one, like a storm, like the ocean whipped up by the winds of one."

"Oh," said Abhay, shaking his head. "That's Rakshastal, Lake of Rakshasas; made when the Asura Ravana prayed there to Lord Shiva and shortly afterward proceeded to kidnap Sita and have Lord Ram," he leaned forward to place his arms around Lord Hanuman's shoulders, "Come to slay him."

Now hc could see it. Ira's eyes were burning with rage, simmering and smoldering with the fires of the soul, which hungered to raze Abhay to ashes. But her face was still blank, as if her mind remembered who Abhay was, and how she cared for him. "At least it is a lake," she said, "That was hallowed by the sheer devotion of one who loved the Lord Shiva, a relic of undying love to the Lord. And you, son of Parashuram, most loyal follower of Devas and opponent of Asuras, would be dead or reduced to madness had it not been for the wildness of Asuras."

They glared at each other, like two flaming stars blazing, radiating the energy of their ancestors, as they strove with each other for lordship over a galaxy.

Then Ira shuddered, quaked, heaved, like a mountain stirring; Abhay did this too, continuing to meet her gaze; then there was a chuckle, a soft laugh; and then they were guffawing, their laughter roaring as it echoed across the valley and filled the air with their joy and mirth.

They held on to each other for support, so they wouldn't fall off Lord Hanuman.

There was a cloud before them, like one of *maya*; they hadn't seen it earlier, but now there it was, shimmering and shrouding the air and their sight to the mountain.

Ira stared at it. This was…ultimate *maya*. No, not the sorcery of some demon or mage or would-be enchanter. This was *maya* itself; the art in the use of its maker, the art as it was fashioned, as it was created in the depths of time. Things came to her mind, things she had not noticed earlier; why was time flowing the opposite way? The sun had been setting, right? Then why had they had daylight for so long, in which they could see all the colors of the plains?

But what was the *maya* veiling?

Lord Hanuman extended a fist that struck at and thrust through the illusion. Then the cloud was parted.

There stood before them, in all its glory, illuminated by the midnight-blue sky, the true Kailash Parvat.

It was no frigid, snow-coated, rock. It was…*svarga*.

For all along the mountainside were trees, shining

silver like shafts of lightning bolts, the purest radiance pulsing and shimmering all along their trunks, lustrous in the night.

There were jewels of sapphire and emerald and ruby and diamond in the mountain, jutting out like outcroppings of the limitless life and color of the Universe. Cascading from many ridges were waterfalls, crystal-clear water glowing with many hues, of fluorescent green and deep navy blue and red, that pulsated and flashed like stardust.

There were animals more glorious than any ever seen upon the Earth; there were tigers, pure golden of skin, regally pacing along the ridges. There were Hanuman Langurs, faces of pure black as if charred by the fires of Lanka, the fur of light golden brown. As Abhay and Ira cast their eyes there, it seemed as if animals of all kinds, of all species, feathered and four-legged and with antennae and claws and scales and armor, thronged the silver forest and walked and stirred and made a cacophony upon the midnight-blue slope of the mountain.

There were the openings of caves, devoid of light, new worlds of darkness carved against the lush forest slope, where goodness knows who lived, where goodness knows what great thoughts were conceived, what visions were made and seen of the Universe in the Lord's deepest meditation.

As they looked through the boughs of the trees,

they saw the waters of many more lakes, sloshing, starlight reflected off their turquoise surfaces. It was as if the mountain, though to appearances having a finite size, had an endless breadth of panoramas, a whole new universe to offer in the depths of the home of the one who had hallowed this one.

Lord Hanuman seemed to pause. Then Ira looked down and started. Where was she? She saw nothing except the mountain itself, except the sky awash with thousands of stars, except an empty space beneath them and Abhay, hovering in the air, still holding each other. A space in which nothing could be seen, and yet there was something, something that lay beneath them and soothed their souls, like the shores of an invisible sea, lapped by waves, waves that would bear them somewhere else if they swam out into it.

Lord Hanuman turned to them and smiled.

"Now, you must fulfill your destinies."

Then they stood before one of the lakes. They looked down into the pure waters of Lake Mansarovar, shining with the purest aqua blue in the Universe, clear as the cosmos, going down into eternal depths of bliss and quiet. There were no waves sloshing or rippling; just a single layer of calm and tranquility, upon which they felt their own souls float, float aimlessly into the distance, at home in the heart of the substance from which they were made.

Then there was a twinkling, like the pulsating of

fuzzy star-stuff as the feet of the young and wide-eyed strolled through them. Abhay and Ira looked ahead and saw…

They saw a low-lying crescent moon, like the *Parashu*, except white, glinting in the darkness of the night, as if levitating above the lake.

Then, flowing from it were waterfalls of the night, pure black and yet contrasting with the night sky. There were beads, like little dark moons strung together on a bead in the sky, hanging in complete stillness. Then they noticed something: a towering shape like a pillar of fire in the night; for though it looked just like a silhouette, it seemed to radiate heat and energy like flame, its broad body branching out smoothly into three points.

It was a trident. Towering out from the water, a shadow in the night, absorbing all the light and all of Abhay and Ira's thought and being into the depths of its make.

Something gripped Abhay and Ira; their souls awakened and throbbed and surged deep in their beings, filling them with the flaming desire to meet this form, to behold the glory of the Lord. They dove into the water, and, with it neck-high, swam on. Ira broke forth with mighty strokes, her hair billowing around her in her desperation, soaked by the water.

Abhay watched her go forth, like another shadow into the night, and felt his heart sink, as his body did too, like a deadweight, lost in the waters of paradise as he quested for an even higher one. He saw only beauty around him; the sky full of stars, the glowing aqua blue water, the visions of holy objects in the distance, but still felt like he was drowning. He had never known how to swim, and as he thrashed, as he kicked furiously, his eyes saw darkness as he went under bit by bit.

Then he stopped. *You don't need to do this.* It was a voice, of lucidity, of knowledge, that guided his soul and raised it up from the depths of confusion.

He raised himself out of the water and felt the soles of his bare feet touch hard rock, scraping at it and gashing it, a throb of pain. Then he looked up.

There, far away, on the horizon, was Mount Kailash. *That was just a vision. Just a sign. All of it. You must make the journey yourself. You must go to Mount Kailash and meet Lord Shiva.*

Then he forgot the pain. He forgot Ira. He forgot the tablet, the prophecy, himself, as he stood straight, shaking in the cold waters and frigid air, and took the first step.

He soldiered on, into the night…and then found himself on the banks of the lake again. He was next to a craft as tall as him. A cylindrical one, of a pure, silver-gray metal like the make of asteroids, burning with a steady, deep light like a fire.

He turned and saw many like this one, on the shores of the lake, forming a ring around it. He could see them even in the distance, distant little flames blazing in the darkness.

He heard a faint gasp behind him. He turned and saw Ira, her face just visible through the darkness and her wild hair, which was strewn all about her face. "Ira…."

"Sshhhh!" she said, and Abhay saw her eyes light up with thrill as she lifted a finger to her lips and quivered with barely suppressed. Exhilaration.

"These are the *vimanas.*"

A voice boomed out in the night; it was...like the blaring of Vishnu's conch, like the rumbling of thunder, like the pulsating of stars, like the singing of birds, like the unfurling of flowers, like the falling of rain, like Abhay chanting *Om Namah Shivaaya* in the dark at Trimbakeshwar…like the sound of the Universe.

Abhay and Ira turned and saw, seated upon the ground in *yogic* posture, legs folded, hands placed upon the knees, Lord Shiva.

His body was that of a dark man, jet black and yet shining like the interstellar cosmic night. There was a crescent moon in his matted hair, locks flowing from it like waterfalls. A bead was around his neck, like twenty-seven dark moons attached in the sky. A deep blue, the blue of Abhay's sword at Pampa Sarovar, pulsated and glowed in his throat. His face was…perfect, with deep black eyes that shone like oceans of bliss and compassion, with the shut lid of a third one above them. Abhay saw, as if coming out of the darkness of the night, four other faces, each of them identical to the first. Then there were ten arms, flowing forth from Lord Shiva's body like his soul was unfurling more and more of its beauty, rivers that danced out. They held wondrous objects that glowed in the night, radiating energy, too dazzling and diverse, shaped from the most primal cosmic elements and forces, for Abhay to make out all of them; but he saw a blazing, pure orange flame like the core of a star, a golden scroll rippling like the folds of a cloud of nectar, a knife flashing with a metal that glinted with a metal even more gray. A tiger skin, waxing a pure golden with black stripes, was draped across his chest.

Abhay and Ira felt as if their *atmans* were leaving their body and soaring into the eternal heights of the *brahman*, of consciousness, where they belonged. Abhay felt as if this body, this shoddy work of shape and form and texture, was nothing more than the broken frame, to hold his soul, to hold the Lord Shiva inside him. Tears gushed forth from his face, like they never had, overwhelmed by love for this being, who was so far above and yet was the whole Universe. He prostrated himself. No *mantras*, no words, no gestures, seemed to have prepared him for this moment.

"Om…O Lord…"

Then at last he sighed.

"I am sorry, Lord," said Abhay. His voice was cold

and stale, like one who was defeated. "I gave up in the lake, not brave enough to even swim for the love of your infinite self."

"And I," said Ira, "am sorry for following illusion, for following shadows and play of light, while you were here all the time, awaiting us."

Shiva raised his right palm. As they gazed upon its pure surface, it seemed to stroke their souls and stop it, bidding it calm down and accept the call of their creator, to accept that they had come to their maker's home and that only quiet was tolerated here.

They were silent. Then Shiva spoke, and it was as if the Universe spoke, telling them of fate and of the waxing and waning of *yugas* and their destinies.

"The two of you," he said, "Are destined to save your world. You have come here to the place where you will give battle to Kali Asura and foil his efforts to cast darkness across the Earth. Be at ease! Be at peace! For you have come, in your language, home. Home to me, who has watched you since you were born, even in the depths of my *samadhi*; home to yourself, for all souls are made by me, and I am in all souls; home to your fate, for it is here that it will be sealed, by your deeds."

Then he turned his glance to Ira, and it felt like the greatest, most venerable, being in the Universe, but also the one she loved the most in the depths of her soul, was gazing upon her.

"You followed illusion. So, you say! But Ira, as you

have yourself said, life is an illusion. I have cast my *maya* upon all of you- the veils, the impurities- so that your *atman* may have a way of living in the real world of *samsara*, of death and rebirth. I am an illusion; I am but Rudra, one of the three forms I, Shiva, take when I reside in the creation of Brahma. Moreover, illusion is your calling; illusion is your power. *Maya*- the powers and the Asura herself- run in your blood. Having such powers and thus chasing my *maya* make you not a withered, failed tree; you have roots that run deep, and in these roots is the might that will enable you to shake Kali Asura by his."

Ira looked up in shock, but also in a sense of peace, as if all was happening as it was meant to; Lord Shiva knew everything about her, everything about her thoughts, but now as he spoke, it seemed natural.

Then he turned to Abhay. "And you, Abhay, have the *atman* of the Lord Vishnu in you; the same that lived as Lord Ram, as Parashuram, your father, and as many others to bring justice to this world and heal it with Lord Hari's will and power. Your father did penance to me for thousands of years, starving himself, denying himself even breath, to win his *parashu*, with which he saved your life, though he lost his. You are of a lineage of warriors, of those who strive against the darkness and against travails of all kinds to uphold the spirit of preservation, of divine triumph, when all is lost. You followed your will, your strength, which said that a march into the darkness would bring you to Lord Shiva."

"Neither of you," he proclaimed, "Could ever be Kalki on your own. One is a *Deva* and is duped by illusion. The other is an Asura of *maya* and is laid low by brute strength and power."

"But that is what Kalki means," said Abhay suddenly. Ira looked at him, shocked; for she heard not Abhay, but the Lord Shiva himself, continuing the Lord's exalted thoughts.

Then she felt it rise in her too, the power of her mother, the power of her *atman*, the power of Lord Shiva.

She reached out with both hands and held Abhay's, tightly, finishing the sentence.

"Warring against the dark together."

The Lord Shiva smiled, with the smile of a creator who has seen his children display the power he had blessed them with, with the smile of one who sees the fate of the world before him and finds only bliss in it.

Then Abhay and Ira remembered- they remembered the tablet, the prophecy, the purpose for which they had embarked on the quest and come here. Abhay reached into his pocket and produced it, but it was as if they both held it as one, handing it over to Shiva not as if they were passing some physical object, but placing the heart of the Universe where it belonged. For in that hour, the tablet transformed, lifted from the mystical, shimmering form Abhay had known and held in awe into something greater, the iridescence of dazzling shades of blue and green streaming forth from its edges like aurora that kindled something deep in their souls, and bequeathed to them some secret knowledge, some secret affinity with the essence of all being.

Then it passed into Shiva. He did not extend his arms, but it seemed to just merge into his being, the colors all mixing into a nebulous, unrecognizable mixture that matched Lord Shiva's color.

He spoke, and his voice was grave with the gravity of the great cosmic blackness as if he was bequeathing important tidings.

"There has been a great war here on Kailash. The Devas and the forces of Kali Asura have rained fire and tempest and wrath upon each other. But all that did was buy time with insignificant skirmishes that are dwarfed by the momentousness of your task."

"What do we do now?" asked Abhay.

"Await your fate," said Lord Shiva. "Do as you were bidden earlier today: have faith in fate, faith in your faith, and faith in yourself."

Then he was gone, the Lord's manifestation going back to reside in his true self.

NINE

Time slowed as they turned toward each other and saw in their eyes and felt in their souls, the divine energies radiating from each of them. A few minutes earlier, both had looked worn-out; Abhay stumbling along, body and hair drenched, eyes pale from fatigue; and while Ira's eyes had shone with wildness and the desire to discover Lord Shiva, she too was soaked, and she had seemed small, lost in the maze of illusion and in the shadows of the night.

Now, though, as they glanced at each other and lay down beside the lake, they felt only their power: the essence of their souls, pulsating with the power of Lord Vishnu and Maya, merging with each other, in a great dance of *shaktis*, the deep blue fire along Abhay's unsheathed blade emerging in the night, and snaking around the deep pink flame that had risen from Ira's chest. They saw in those flames and in each other's faces the warmth of that night by the flame in the forest and let their works of magic and conjuring swirl around each other. Each was separate, blazing with its distinct flame, but yet nourishing itself with the glow of the other, wrapping around each other before coming undone again.

"Abhay..." said Ira.

"Yes?"

There was a pause.

"We've been through so much."

Abhay nodded. Not much more needed to be said; for upon Ira's face, illuminated by the aqua light of the lake and the midnight-blue of the skies, glimmered the colors of blood spurting from a cut throat, of forest green and gushing blue, of a crepuscular gray and black, streaked by the hot-white that felled Parushram, of the radiant pink of her *maya* flame, of the blue of the eternal skies, of the golden and red of Lord Hanuman's face, of the pure color of Lord Shiva, serene in the darkness.

They looked up at the stars together, their flames of blue and pink-orange dancing in a show of light and divine power before them, crackling and swirling beneath the stars. "Abhay, our parents will come back, right?"

It seemed out of place in the mystical land of Lord Shiva, when they'd learned long back that their true parents were gods. But some things never changed.

He wrapped his arm around Ira's back, as she had done to him the night by the fire.

"Yes."

Then Abhay started. "The....the tablet? It's right here! What the...."

He did not point out that they had already given it to Shiva, for he knew deep inside that the Lord still had it. He would always have it, and in some fundamental sense had always had it.

Ira laughed, and her laugh to Abhay was like the gushing of water in a stream, like the twinkling of the stars in the sky, as it soothed his heart.

"Here it is. Maya, maya, maya. Life is always an illusion, my righteous Deva. And the only true maya is Shiva's."

She showed it to him. The tablet itself seemed less a solid object than something that was being projected into their midst, its edges blurring and crackling. The runes, the Harappan pictograms, were all gone. No longer did any fish swim, trees stand, rivers flow, etched into the clay; all that was left was the thrashing, tempestuous waters of a lake: dark blue streaked with crepuscular grey in the daylight, a ball of fire incinerating a line of mountains to an ash that coated the skies.

Then there was...Mansarovar; the placid, aqua-blue waters of a lake, a great blade with a blue flame running all along it flashing and hurling the power of the Gods at some great darkness, that caused the lake to ripple and heave like a beast as it grew.

Then the letters were back, gleaming golden as they always had.

Abhay and Ira looked at each other.

"So, me in Rakshastal," said Ira, eyes suddenly fey and misty as they gazed at the skies. "You know, the lake of the villain Ravana and his kin, as you would say."

"And me in Mansarovar," said Abhay, gulping as if swallowing some truth that gave him strength as he took it in but also felt somehow cold. "The boring, sleepy lake of the *Devas*, who there would be none to defend tomorrow if it were not for the wildness and might of the Asuras."

"It fits," said Abhay. "One Asura and one Deva make up Kalki, and each will give battle upon the shores of the lake made for their ancestors. You know, fighting with all the powers of our forefathers and mothers."

Ira nodded. She felt it in her mind, stronger than ever as if her mother were not merely embracing her but had entered her, filling her with her power and love so that she may blaze a trail of triumph through the night to consume Kali Asura tomorrow.

But still, her gaze fell, as if looking down at some truth that felt lower than all the high prophecies and powers but was nonetheless important to her.

"But we'll…be apart in the final fight." She pulled one of the strands of her hair, blown out around her face, across her eyes, as if to hide her worried, fragile eyes. But Abhay reached out and moved it back, to see eyes that were shrunken and yet still, as if pondering some great truth that gave peace but also some cause for gloom. They then lifted, as is finding solace and hope in his presence.

"We'll be apart, but not alone; the bond that binds us in Kalki will keep us together. Remember? Neither of us is Kalki on our own."

"It's like," he said, as he felt Ira move away a little, as if bracing herself for the loneliness of tomorrow, "Your bond with your mother." At that, Ira's gaze lifted, and a new fire shone in her eyes; one that was the pink of her conjured flame, and yet the aqua blue of the lake, and then some entirely different color- a warmth that glowed on her skin, like the flame of some deep love. "You have never 'met' or 'seen' each other- and yet are you not together? Don't you feel her presence in your mind as if she is embracing you, as if she is right next to you, as if she is with you, guiding you and sharing her love and power with her daughter?"

Ira smiled, and it was the smile of one who had been through many journeys, battered by blade and tempest and cold, splattered at times with blood and loss and frigid waters, but still had something to hold onto amidst it all.

"We've been who we are our whole lives, and we will always be."

She turned to him completely, as if ready now to face the future and Abhay's earnest gaze. "You told me that once."

Abhay looked back at her, meeting her eyes, before shaking his head. "So even now, in your moment of philosophical self-realization, you steal my words, Asura?"

"Abhay!" She lifted her hands as if to strike at him but ended up getting lost in his shining eyes and smiled, and laughed as she hugged him from behind instead. "You know," she said, "That's so right, in more ways than I'd understood earlier. Stuff changes, but the core of who we are doesn't change- so our powers, our *atman*, our roots that make us ourselves; and relationships with people that matter don't change. No matter where we are, I am always with my mother and father- my human father. And with you."

Abhay nodded and felt those words strike at some vital part of himself, not shimmering in the air like the stars but settling in the sky and making everything so much more beautiful. The midnight-blue was deep as the deepest part of the ocean, and the lake was pure aqua now, like the poison in Lord Shiva's throat. As he turned a little to look at Ira, he saw not what he'd usually see- the wildness of Ira, either amplified and flared up by the thrill of adventure or dulled by exhaustion. He saw Ira, hair billowing about and smothering his neck in a soft embrace, face at peace as it glowed in the light of stars and the lake, eyes open wide in wonder and yet settled, as if calm.

But he also saw something else: someone so different from him, literally the opposite- wild, restless, at times overbearing, impatient. Hell, in the past few days, Parashuram had literally told them that; all the gods, Lord Shiva himself, had told them that in their souls they were contrasting, belonging to two races that were sworn enemies over millennia of endless strife.

"Yes, we've been who we are our whole lives, but that's almost always different from what we've thought it was all these years."

Ira didn't say anything; there was no hasty question, no frown. She just inclined her head at Abhay, as it shimmered in a ghostly glow of aquamarine, the aqua of the waters and the blue of the skies merging in a glorious hue that illuminated her face, eyes sparkling with questioning but also with warmth.

"We always thought we were different; you know, I was the smart guy who read and talked and thought about fancy stuff, and you were the wild girl who loved only to feel the wind blow on her back as she ran in a race. But we were quite similar: we were both young, with mundane lives that had always seemed smaller than us; boring, without life, without soul- indeed, our souls revolted against it, yours thrashing like a storm to break free, and mine whirring with endless visions and a sense of quiet dissatisfaction. Then the ones we loved the most were taken away from us with one knife stroke, and we were thrust out into a world where we were even more lost; lost in all the grand prophecies and gods and...everything," he said, both of them laughing as he swept his hand through the air as if to say he still couldn't believe where they were and all they'd been through. "But we found ourselves, and they were very different from who we thought we were. I wasn't an orphan, alone, without parents, with a chronic fear of loss. I was the son of Parashuram, the incarnation of..."

He stopped as if he hadn't considered this before- "Lord Vishnu, filled with a power I'd never imagined in my wildest fantasies. And you? You weren't without roots, without any past or companionship beyond your father, with a tempestuous soul that didn't fit this world and was at home only in the fury of a storm. We were…"

"We were ourselves," said Ira, smiling, it widening as she saw Abhay's face, frozen as he saw just how simply, predictably, and yet perfectly, that had ended.

"But Abhay," said Ira, holding him closer, and he could feel her hair brushing his cheek now as she leaned forward. "We've found ourselves, yes."

"But perhaps we never would have, if we hadn't found each other."

Time slowed. Time slowed as Abhay and Ira sat in each other's arms, on the shores of Lake Mansarovar, watching the stars burn high above, the water shimmering in their light, alone, though surrounded by the glows from all the vimanas, bright but ghostly against the midnight-blue backdrop.

It felt like forever; a simple moment of togetherness, of warmth, held on the eve of cataclysmic war, perhaps catastrophe; perhaps the last peaceful moment they'd ever have before they were lost in Kali's storm, with the rest of a godforsaken planet. Along the way, they noticed that the tablet flickered and shimmered all over, before fading once again into the background of the skies, never to be seen again, even in illusion, by anyone but the Lord Shiva himself.

***

Then, at some point- perhaps by Shiva's *maya*, Abhay felt like he was sitting elsewhere, though the touch of Ira warmed his whole body as he sat, full of bliss and comfort, on the banks of Mansarovar. Most of the *vimanas* had turned off their lights, though the radiance from the lake illuminated the metallic, gray, forms of some of them. Then a thought arose, like a breaking wave amidst all the tranquility: he'd called himself an *avatar* of the Lord Vishnu, right? As he gazed upon the lake and lost himself in those waters, he seemed to sink into them, and the meaning of his words did too. He'd thought of himself, even after everything, even after all that self-discovery, as the son of Parashuram- a great man, a formidable, mighty *avatar* of the Lord Vishnu. But to think he was the living manifestation of a God… that…was just a bridge too far- no, a Universe too far.

Then there was movement.

One of the *vimanas* flickered to life. The lights came on, and not only glowed like small fires but enveloped the form in a blaze, a flaming halo that covered and gushed forth from its body. It felt like it burned, a fire raged in his soul, pining for the glory of being an inferno in the darkness. Then that flame thrashed out with its pulsating tendrils as if razing out from the midnight blue sky its soul, the core of all that color, of all that being, and manifesting all its beauty by Abhay's side.

Then there it was. A dark being, as dark as the starry skies, and yet the skin imbued with a deeper darkness; that of the cosmos, that of the void of the universe before its creation; one with Lord Shiva's, and yet unique in some way Abhay could not explain, sucking in his mind, his soul, his whole being, before his sight wandered to the other parts of the figure.

There was a crown on his head, like the Sun, with a halo of golden peacock feathers speckled with red and green extending out from a central spire like that of a temple, starting with a broad rounded base before narrowing into a golden pinnacle spoke, with the feather of a peacock fluttering in the wind at the peak.

This golden, lustrous, crown, shining with the brilliance of a sun, was inlaid with gems like the cores of stars- one green, elliptical one, like a *vimana*, and another red one, like the Lord Hanuman's eyes. There were four arms, extending out like the spirals of deep-blue galaxies in the night. The upper left held a pure white conch tipped with gold; the lower left held a golden mace, with a thick head, round like the globe of the Earth; the lower right held a blooming, bright pink lotus flower, upon a thin green stalk; and the upper right…Abhay felt all the golden spokes thrusting at and piercing every old vision in his mind of a wheel running into the night, that had in some way represented all his fears, all his thoughts, all his fate. His sight, illuminated by the brilliance, glided in awe along the smooth surface of the pure golden disc at the center of it all, completing the…the...

Lord Vishnu smiled. "Yes, Abhay. This is the Kaalchakra. The Wheel of Time. Now, the Wheel is not moving for it is still in anticipation, in the knowledge that it is on the threshold, on the brink of a cliff that falls into a bottomless darkness, but upon which life and warmth remain."

"It is the Wheel of the Universe, the *yugas* spinning, flowing into each other- creation flowing into destruction over an epochs-long revolution from truth and order to darkness and chaos. I know it is one you revere and have had visions of. Such it is with all who are wise and still know something of the Vedas in this unholy, dark age."

"My…My Lord!" said Abhay, feeling all of his senses fading, overwhelmed and blasted by a cosmic wind, by all the force of the Universe, his being running with the rivers of the galaxies, of the flow of the Kaalchakra, of the thoughts of Vishnu…of his own thoughts.

He collapsed and was prostrate at the feet of the Lord, which he could see, shimmering with a deep blue-black like the cosmos, twinkling with what looked like stars within, as if the Lord himself was the cosmos. Then he felt a touch upon his forehead, like that of the essence of creation soothing him; but also, like the touch of something he'd known all along, as if his own soul, his own self, were reaching out and meeting his mind at last.

"My Lord," said Abhay, thick tears dripping down his face, "Why don't I feel a oneness with you? Why am I still trapped in my body, with this mind, in this frail form, if I am truly one of your lineage inside?"

There was a pause. Then, it came, like the strumming of celestial melodies that calmed and cascaded through his soul.

"This Wheel," he said, "is also the Sudarshan Chakra, my weapon. But tomorrow, this will not come soaring through the skies to slice off Kali Asura's head. You will. You know why you can't merge into me, Abhay?

Why you can't break free from your physical form, return to me, and channel all my limitless power into defeating Kali Asura? Because he would win, because only you can vanquish the darkness. You *need* your mind, Abhay, troubled and burdened by the tumults of this world though it may be. You need that rage, that wrath at the slaying of your beloved grandfather who was all you ever had, his throat cut in the dead of night by some craven, filthy, coward who licked Kali Asura's feet all his life. You need that love for this world, for your grandfather, for your father and mother, for Ira, for Lord Shiva, for me, for the power coursing through your veins and the flame of Shiva pulsing along your blade, to have that desperation to save it, to pour forth the blaze of your soul and nourish it with abhorrence for the infernal Asura, before you raze him to ashes Thus, it is by being who you are in the final battle, you will triumph, and turn the Kaalchakra, becoming the only one besides the *devas*, with Ira, to ever turn it."

***

Ira remained there, lying by the glowing waters of Lake Mansarovar. She'd fallen asleep, hadn't she? Now she was awake, her eyes dimly taking in all the lights and colors of her surroundings.

But she'd seen, conjured, and unveiled too many illusions over the past few days to be surprised. No, she knew, with the depths of her being, that this was not just another of those; this was not even like the illusions of Lord Shiva she'd seen on Mount Kailash, the most skillful in the Universe. This was like the work of the ultimate master of illusion, one who was synonymous with *maya*, who had all the essence of the craft in her soul, an essence that flowed into her daughter and filled her with belonging, with love, as she lay on the banks of Lake Mansarovar, the purest, most real body of water in existence, in *maya* form.

It looked perfect, but almost too perfect; the placid, pure waters twinkled with starlight and the flaming orbs of the vimanas blazed in the distance, in perfect harmony, of uniform size, like a swarm of fireflies; the hills on afar rippled and undulated like a series of dark waves.

But true perfection was the sheer peace of love that enveloped it all. Ira felt herself embraced; embraced by the night itself, a touch that was warmed by the fires of the stars and *vimanas*, and deepened by the purity of the *brahman*, of pure consciousness, of undiluted love and bliss. It was directed at the whole Universe and yet entirely at Ira, as if the wielder of all this *shakti* wanted to give it all to Ira, to harness and wield herself.

Then she saw it. Amidst all the aqua blue before her, all the midnight-blue of the skies, all the fires of the *vimanas*, there was a presence. It felt to her as if it contained the essence of them all and of the most profound depths of the Universe.

She remembered Danu from Pampa Sarovar, a whirling, gushing being of many waves and currents. This was similar, except with a brilliant, icy, blue, and purity like the clearest crystals that shimmered with a heavenly resplendence, a resplendence that dazzled her eyes but also comforted her soul. She thought she saw swirls of hair, radiant eyes,

It swaddled with the same embrace as her mother's voice had; it was as infinite, but not in an empty way, for it was imbued with a love just as infinite as its nature.

"Ira."

It was breathed out, and the waters rippled, and the air rustled, and Ira breathed in a breath, saturated with intoxication and love and warmth. She knew it, felt it at last, in a sense deeper than any over the past few days: her mother was here.

"Maa…Maaa," she said, running forth, and then as she extended her reach, she perceived herself levitate and feel her mother, boundless energy, crackling and gushing all over her arms.

"I love you…I love you so much," she breathed, inhaling the exhilarating draught of Maya and exhaling her soul, inhuming it with the holy flame of her mother.

"I miss you. All this time you have been in me, and I have been in you, and I belong with you Maa, and I am you…but still, it is as if I have somehow not been with you in a close sense, in a physical sense; for my mind, my heart, longs to embrace you."

"Then come, *putri.*" This time, it was not an ethereal breath, but a voice, full of melody and illusion and magic and love…full of *maya.*

The next few hours were like none Ira had ever experienced, except perhaps her favorite times with her father; and yet, it was something more, for it was that night with her mother that she found her true self, and Maya prepared her daughter for what was to come.

***

The next day, Abhay awoke to a very different Mansarovar. Gone was the ethereal aqua glow, the midnight-blue skies, and the fires of the *vimanas* burning in the night. This was a landscape of cragged rocks, ascending to undulating peaks of snow in the distance, where the *vimana's* silver was lustrous with that otherworldly metallic glow, where the waters of Mansarovar were a still pure blue in the sunlight.

Abhay felt something in his heart tighten, as if bracing himself for some great tumult, before it subsided. Then there was a stillness, a quiet inside, the peace of self-assurance and strength. Then it seemed as if the rays of the sun broke upon his soul and set it ablaze with a fire that spread like a flame that could immolate the world, but now smoldered with a special kind of wrath, as if the embers of his soul had been ignited, a wrath directed at....at....

At the shadow that he saw casting itself on the peaks in the distance as if a dark planet was passing the Earth; at the stirring in the lake's waters, as if they were gusted by an evil wind, tranquil waters rippling with an unease that struck right at Abhay like a cold blade. The *vimanas* were silent witnesses to this disturbance, their stolid grey surfaces, once feeling magical and beautiful, now feeling only grim and pale.

Then there it was. There was Bhaya, the long-fanged, red-eyed, ghastly phantom in the night. There was the *mayavi* shade of Mahabali, with his bloodied, gashed face. Then last of all, thunder boomed in the skies- the thunder with which Kali Asura had struck his father and felled him from the heavens. The skies were rent apart, and all the land was shrouded in a swirling, thick storm, as if engulfed by a tornado, by some great tempest that bore darkness and pestilence. The clear blue skies were wreathed by dark clouds, in the depths of which there was the flashing of thunder.

Then it appeared. An apparition of the pure night, conjured from all the most infernal, depraved, concoctions of the Asuras who sought to cast their blight across the Earth.

It was Kali Asura. It was Bhaya- the same dark, crepuscular form, with red eyes like blood moons and fangs like icicles in a frigid cave. But it was also Jara-a faded form, with dried, wrinkled skin like that of a decayed being. It was also Danu, imbued with the pure blue hues of Pampa Sarovar and the flash of pink from the lotuses.

Then he spoke, and it was like a voice, an emanation that echoed through the walls of the darkest chasms, pounded upon the walls of the fragile minds of all the world's creatures, threatening to level them like a gargantuan asteroid, and then....and then came the darkness, unknown, endless, pervasive, all-knowing, and about to swallow Abhay.

"I am all these, Abhay. I am the one you need to fear."

Then it pulsated, throbbed, crackling with the charge of all the Universe's lightning- a bolt. It glowed with the same cold, ethereal light of the *vimana's* make, and yet in its depths was the luster, the fervor, the electric power of lightning.

Then Kali Asura's arm, an ever-changing, tempestuous mirage of myriad flashing colors and shapes, hefted the *vajra* at Abhay. As it hurtled through the air, pulsing with limitless power, crackling with the energy of a thousand suns, Abhay felt it. He felt as if he were standing on the Earth, insignificant, beneath a black sky like the void of Kali Asura- the primal darkness and evil that would shroud the Earth in the Kali Yuga. Then there was a boom, a deep sound, as if emanated, exuded from the depths of the Universe, but one that resounded through and rent all the Earth. There was a flash of lightning, a blinding white radiance in the mirk that told him he would be felled, incinerated, and reduced to ash, that would be the residue of not only his funeral, but also that of his father, Lord Vishnu, and the whole world.

But as it struck out, its forked shaft thrusting at him like the specter of devastation, he raised his arm; and all the pulsing, primal power of Lord Shiva pulsated through it, like all the might of all the *devas*.

Then he was again there, by the waters of Lake Mansarovar; and the sight of the placid, blue waters, the rolling hills and peaks in the distance, the *vimanas* standing like silent but heavenly spectators to the ultimate battle of all time. The vimanas stirred, fired up by something, as if the *vimanas* had fired up the divine fuel in themselves, and were taking off and firing back at Kali in his soul.

There was his sword- the golden letters on its hilt were glowing like the lights of all the stars in the Universe, as the blue flame gushed all over its surface like the supreme *shakti* of Lord Shiva, as if the power that infused the mountains, the lake, the *vimanas*, the skies, had poured forth, thrashing with the wrath of the Gods. Abhay's hand moved as if of its own accord, slashing the mighty sword into the path of the oncoming *astra*.

The *vajra* astra was torn asunder when it struck the blade, reduced to a few disparate, faded charges sputtering into silence, the sparks playing across the blade of the sword.

Then Kali Asura's eyes glowered. The fires deep in them raged with the fury of those who were forsaken, who were born in the shadow that bred in the twilight away from all the glory of the Gods.

Then there was a grin. The fangs flashed with the brilliance of the *vajra* itself, but a colder form of it; as if eons-old frost had coated it, gathering in the frigid, desolate caves in the darkness that bred the might of Kali Asura.

"*Bhaya,*" said Kali Asura. His voice was like… like…like if the monster had spoken in the night at the forest. It coagulated Abhay's veins, shivered his lungs until they were shriveled and lifeless; blew away the fire of his soul, of his father, like the cold gust that could rival the might of the *Devas*.

"You have tasted *Bhaya*…when?" Kali grinned, and in those suddenly lidless eyes and in the shards of his teeth and fangs, he saw…his grandfather. He was sprawled against the wall, his face ghostly pale in the spectral moonlight. There was a shadow looming over him, back turned to Abhay. Then a blade emerged from it, a knife, like the fangs of Kali, which pulsated with the eerie luminance of alien worlds, of a shard of moonlight rising in the night of existence. Then it thrust at his grandfather, right into his throat. He croaked, and his outreached palms, as if grasping for hope, for salvation, went still. The form stiffened, the pale visage of death shrouding him before all was plunged into darkness.

Kali's grin was now greater than ever. His eyes were wild, wild with the thrill the maddened got from tormenting others and seeing them crumble, seeing them cower in terror and writhe with grief. Abhay saw it. In those eyes he saw the night, heard the shrill cry of his grandfather from another room as the Gods whisked him away; he heard the crash of thunder that felled his father, plummeting helplessly from the sky. In them he saw the blaze that would raze to ashes the entire world, burning in one flame the hopes for the resurrection of those he loved, and many other lives, and all the hope for the renewal of the Earth, and all the ascendancy of the *devas*, and justice and peace.

In them he saw…death. In them, he saw grief. In them, he saw the slow burning of his whole world, the blackened corpse of his grandfather, the Earth reduced to a charred, malformed pulp.

He was in a void, reaching out into the darkness for…for…something. For life. For love. For hope, for a home amidst this driftless, empty existence, where Kali had triumphed.

Then there was a ray; a ray of light from above, piercing right through the bottomless darkness.

It was as if his soul was lifted through it on a vessel, and then he was in a firmament, in an infinite haven from the darkness.

Then he felt that tender yet mighty grip holding his hand, and saw the scarred face of Parashuram, a prodigious gash left by the *vajra*; and Abhay felt the sheer agony of the force of millions of suns blazing into his skin.

Then there was a surge of light from the emptiness, and Parashuram was wreathed in an all-consuming, all-illuminating halo that shimmered with an ethereal radiance and sparkled with a cosmic flame.

But he was not alone. Beside him was another being. Abhay's eyes melted as he saw her, but that was as much out of love as out of the searing heat of her form.

For there, robed in red and gold, the peace of the heavens and of deliverance, the shimmering radiance of the stars, the beautiful depths and colors of love, suffused from a form.

"*Putra,*" said a voice, that susurrated and yet reverberated through the fabric of the firmament like the voice of a goddess.

"Maa…" he reached forward frantically, trying to touch his mother, trying to feel the one whose presence he had so missed in his life.

"Go and cleanse this world of its blight. Go. Do it for your grandfather. For your father. For me. For the world."

Then it was all gone. He sighed and it was as if his mother and father breathed all through him. He was calm. At last, he looked up at Kali Asura, and he saw in him no power- only…only…infernal, accursed, abominable night, a craven coward who hid in the shadows from the glory of the God's creation, who used their powers for depraved sins when their kin such as Ira and Maya had used them for good. He saw in him only…

The enemy of Lord Shiva, whose temple he would destroy. The enemy of Lord Vishnu, whose manifestation on the Earth they had slain. The enemy of his grandfather, an innocent, loving man whose life they had stolen away in the darkness of night.

He sensed the devilish grin, the glint in those eyes, fade. A shroud came over Kali's face, as if a frost had come upon it, dimming those glowering red suns to faint, faded lamplights. The deep black, like the endless void of the night, had weakened somewhat, fading to a gray, as if a few stars, though new and unsure of their color, had come into existence, and it was awash with their light. The eyebrows seemed to arch a bit, and the triumphant expression began to evaporate, as the realization dawned on him that Abhay had managed to conquer his fear.

Abhay concentrated. His form was not worth looking at, for it was an infernal, accursed phantom conjured from all the most debased darkness in the Universe.

Kali and his minions were also his enemies, for Kali

Asura and his filthy demon brethren and spawn had taken from him all that he held dear, all that he loved, all that he thought he was.

Then Abhay gasped. For he saw…nothing. There was just a silhouette, the shadows of the fangs, the legs, the head, like mirages, like the faded shapes left after a great radioactive storm.

It was all…illusion. He remembered something from a conversation with Ira long ago:

Life was just an illusion. Only the *brahmaan*, the pure consciousness of the Universe, and all the *atmans*, the souls that were a part of it, were real.

This Kali…he had no soul.

But Abhay did.

Then the blade of Shiva pulsed, a cosmic, deep blue flame thrashing and blazing and pulsing all along it. Abhay advanced, and as he did so, he remembered his father, as he faced off against this demon in the skies. In his strides was all of Parashuram's strength and vigor, as he bounded forth at the depraved, barbaric demon, the blade crackling with sparks of flame and electricity like a lightning bolt as he thrust it at Kali.

***

Ira stood there, an island of stillness before the wrath, the raging tempest of Rakshastal, gray waters thrashing.

But even that stillness was illusory. Inside her mind, the waves and the strokes of lightning that now crashed upon the lake and rent the mountain air were fermenting a storm, a storm that writhed with fury and threatened to wreck it.

She remembered the last time she'd felt like this. She remembered falling in the forest forward as the bloodied, limp form of her father, pale in the moonlight, appeared in her mind, and she drowned in a flood of anguish and bereavement and rage.

She remembered watching thunder crash and the form of Parashuram fall from the heavens and feeling a sense of awe and dread deep in her soul as if she'd just witnessed some great, primal power.

And she remembered…she remembered…

The darkness and death. When? From…from somewhere very, very far from the bliss and conjured pink flames and shimmering, embracing warmth of love that was her mother.

"*Pralaya,*" said a voice, carrying its shadow, its weight like the fey, ominous pulsations of energy across the lake like a dark moon looming over already troubled seas, and then consuming Ira, an insignificant form in that umbra. "The Universe began with what, Ira? Not creation, no. With *Mahapralaya*- the Great Dissolution. There was nothing, only an emptiness, an infinite void. So pure, oh so pure..."

Ira felt something, like the serrated, sharp blade

of a knife being grated across her mind. There was…a vision. A vision without sight. A vision of a void, as if the void was her mind, as if the void was her.

"Your father would be ashamed of you, little enchantress of *Mayavi.*" Then there he was, as if the necromancer who had brought forth this darkness from the long dead had finally appeared. It was a figure robed all in black, with a face wrought from the darkest, most infernal phantoms of the night. There were two eyes, deep red like suns tainted by the blood of the lonely souls that orbited it. It radiated a black halo, as if emanating, like clouds of darkness spilling out of Kali's soul to engulf the world.

"The prophecy says you are the daughter of destruction and illusion- of Pralaya and Maya. Why did you never wonder about your father?"

Then Ira felt something new. The night was not a wall of evil, hideous and abominable, meant to be cast away by the radiance of her illusion-unveiling power. It was a whole new world, where answers awaited, where glory awaited, where she would be part of the insurrection against oppression and the unfurling of the wrath and power of Asuras.

She felt the darkness pulse and gush through her veins and body, and tendrils of blackness shot up and swirled from her fingers and arms.

Then it was there. It was there like it had been when she'd seen her father's bloodied body, and been filled with the call of her soul, leaping out her window. It was there like it had been the night she'd willed a flame to come, and the deep pink-orange fire of *maya* had blazed for her and Abhay in the cold and wind. It was there like it had been last night, when she'd been lain before Lake Mansarovar, comforted by the radiance of the waters and the stars and her mother's love.

It was her mother, back, an ocean of calm and love and bliss that filled Ira and once again made her aware of who she was, of who her mother was; and that meant the Universe to her.

Suddenly, she felt a flame, an opal-blue fiery light, shoot up from her palms as she opened them. It gushed forth from her hands and swirled, and in the flowing path of the fire, painting a spiral galaxy in the air. She felt her soul stirring in every tendril, in every spark, in every pulsation of color; she felt it shake and unfurl as the blue galaxy raced at the dark cloud that was Kali Asura, and then dance; dance the dance of destruction, of unveiling, of casting away and immolating the darkness of Kali, consuming it in a Universal flame.

Then the flames raged. In them, she felt her spirit's wrath at the death of her father, his blood shed in a stormy, shadow-wreathed night, throat slit by a craven cowardly beast like this one.

They raged against the night, and blazed it away, for it had never been there before, save in memory, in imagination, in fear, festering in the decay of the world;

a world now cleansed of that perfidious power by the *shakti* of Maya.

***

Abhay heaved the blade at the dark form of Kali, who parried the blow with his own blade, the sparks formed by the meeting of the two blades crackling like lightning in the darkness. Something had changed. Abhay did not dare turn his gaze from his foe, but he could feel that Ira had triumphed, that her *maya* had weakened the powers of darkness. While earlier Abhay had been parrying Kali Asura's blows with exertion, now he could feel the momentum shifting in the duel.

Feint, lunge, block, side-step.

The muscle memory forged by years of practice in the dojo fused with powers that coursed through his being, powers beyond his comprehension, propelled him forward.

Gone was Kali Asura's smirk.

Gone was his taunting.

Gone was his goading.

As Abhay struck out again with his glowing blade and Kali took a step back, Abhay realized something that came as a shock.

Kali Asura was afraid.

He had hoped to use his powers of illusion and brute force together to destroy Kalki. Ira had robbed him of his powers of magic and Abhay was now besting him in the battle of blades. Truly, together they could triumph where either one of them alone would have perished.

Abhay screamed and lunged, calling out for strength to the one who had blessed this blade.

"Har Har Mahadev!"

It struck, with a world-rending crash that resounded like the colliding of galaxies, sending oceans of blue incandescent electric charge pulsing and throbbing and burning all along Kali's body. It was like a star had detonated inside the infernal, depraved black hole of Kali, and as it blew apart, Abhay saw the fragments of the darkness scatter in tatters, feeling now not like a terrifying abomination but the scattering of hollow, lifeless dust that began to drift away with the wind.

Then there was nothing, and yet there was everything; nothing for where Kali's phantom had stood was just the stillness of Lake Mansarovar and the celestial *vimanas*, the emptiness of the heavens, the bliss of the perfect mountains of Shiva rolling in the distance. He felt it awash with a new life, a new peace, as if all of existence had been calmed by the dissolution of Kali. But more important for Abhay was how he felt that while the blast had killed Kali Asura, from the cosmic energy of his strike would be born new lives. He pictured himself in his grandfather's arms, feeling that warm embrace again. He pictured himself in his father's lap by the fireside like he'd been on that last night.

Then Kali was gone.

Abhay felt it, a sudden ocean of bliss, of victory, of ecstasy, swelling up in him, then flowing through his bones and his veins and his lungs, filling all with a peace, that his soul was awash with.

He felt Ira, too; all that wild, thrashing *shakti*, the heat of a heavenly blaze of a powerful spirit that was his kindred soul.

Kalki had triumphed.

Then he felt something else; the tranquil, celestial skies darkened, as if some last shade of darkness had breathed onto them. Then he felt it; the fire faded a bit, the heat in his soul tinged with a bitter frost.

Then a voice rang out; the deep, melodious voice that rung with the beauty of the depths of the cosmos, of the shattering of the *vajra*, of the whistling of the winds of Kailash, of the blasting of Lord Vishnu's conch.

"Abhay, you have triumphed. You have proven the prophecy and fulfilled your destiny as Kalki. Your valor, your belief, and your strength, have been tested. Today, when you cast the Trishul, manifested as your sword, into Kali Asura's heart, you dispelled the demons that you once dreaded with your life- Bhaya, the turning of the *yuga*, Kali. But there is one more test, which will be the death of one of you and Ira. Only one of you may live today. Make your choice."

Abhay took a deep breath, realizing that the choice

was an easy one to make.

***

Not far away, as the waters of Rakshastal calmed, Ira saw Abhay; she saw the person who she'd disregarded in some distant lifetime at school, but then the person who'd accompanied her out into the perilous, treacherous wild of her destiny. The person who'd screamed, with blood-red, anguished eyes, whom she'd put her arms around to comfort after thunder had struck down his father; the one whom she'd held on to as they rode on Devadatta like a gust of divine wind, giving her comfort and keeping her still, even as the grand prophecies and visions threatened to carry her far away. The person who'd been a kindred spirit to her, in whom she'd been able to share the feeling of loss, of fear, which then grew into a shared triumph, a shared resolve, a shared power, a shared bond.

She had been given the same choice, and for her too, the choice was an easy one to make.

Ira spoke without hesitation.

"Let Abhay live."

At the same instant, Abhay spoke.

"Let Ira live."

Then there was silence. Both closed their eyes, bracing themselves, reserving all of their might to endure the next few moments.

But nothing happened.

Before both of them appeared a single figure. They'd beheld him the previous day, but now he was…simpler. His skin was coated all in ash, *rudraksha* beads around his neck. The third eye was shut firmly, and the other two looked on in love and warmth. There was but one head, with matted hair, imbued with all the beauty of the Universe, shimmering with deep blue all over. He only had one pair of hands, and his right did not hold the Trishul, but on its index finger spun the *Sudarshan Chakra*. Briefly, Abhay saw Vishnu appear by Shiva's side, and the *chakra* switched hands to the Deva.

"It was but a test. Both of you have proven yourself as Kalki, and by discovering who you are and all you are capable of, you have unleashed the might of the *Devas* on Kali Asura and saved this world and all of existence. You have also shown that you are able to put others ahead of your own self. That is the essence of dharma. Now you may return to your homes and be with your loved ones once more; and live your lives in human society as you did earlier, awaiting the summons that may come."

Then Shiva was gone, as was Vishnu, merging into the backdrop of the mountains and lakes, as if the landscape had been one with them all along.

Then everything around them spun. It all spun like the Kaalchakra gyrating through the dark, whirring on, not the uneasy, unreal spin Abhay had once hallucinated of. It was as if the wheel of time, the Kaalchakra, churned out beauty, love, clarity, dispelling darkness, as a bright, calming, soothing light enveloped both of them.

***

Abhay felt the same old, soft, warm form wrap itself around him, feeling the spectacles rest on his shoulder, the crease in the lips as they smiled, the crease in the eyes as they were brought to the stillness of love and belonging.

"I had the strangest dream, Abhay. It's hard to explain, but it felt like I was far away."

Abhay grinned.

"I had a strange dream too, Dadu, but it's great to be back home, back just the way we were."

Abhay had woken up in his bed, and rushed to his grandfather's room, to see him peacefully asleep on his bed.

Had it all been a dream? Had all the memories that rested in his head just been his imagination? The clock showed that it was the morning after he had discovered the tablet. There was no broken glass, no evidence of the adventures he had been through.

There was also, no trace of the tablet.

Where had it gone?

"What are you thinking of Abhay? You seem lost

in thought."

"Nothing, Dadu," he said, and hugged his grandfather like he never had.

***

Ira was there; in her room, looking upon the Arabian Sea, glimmering with sunlight, still and peaceful. She turned and saw, in the very doorway she'd seen his bloodied, cold body, her father; but this time his form was full of life, awash with vigor and love, beaming as he gazed upon his daughter for the first time in what seemed, inexplicably, like forever.

As she hugged him, she felt her mind snuggled, as if someone had swaddled it with the blanket of love, keeping it safe from the darkness that had raged there in the background for so long.

She realized that though the ride had been wild and allowed her to find out things about herself she'd never dared to imagine, only now was she truly home.

EPILOGUE

School that day was surreal. Abhay kept looking at his friends and classmates, realizing just how glad he was back in the world where he had never really fit in, but which was now strangely comforting. Yet, a part of him missed what he had seen in his dream. Having his powers, having a purpose…having a father.

He passed Ira in the hallway and looked at her, before quickly averting his eyes.

What a dream that had been! One where, of all people, Ira had been the one he had to count on the most. The one he had grown to care about and trust.

After school ended, Abhay left the building along with the other students. He walked away, talking to Vihaan as they moved along.

Just then, as he was on the verge of entering the bus, his ears were filled with a great clamor, voices whispering as if from a great distance. Abhay froze.

It had been no dream.

He looked upwards and saw the sky had been torn open, revealing a huge space with a bright array of colors, yellow and green, red and blue, as the face of Shiva looked down at him. The piercing gaze of Shiva, filled with wisdom and knowledge, the third eye now open and flaming like a blazing sun, transfixed Abhay and jolted him awake from his stupor with one stroke. Beside him was Vishnu, and upon his index finger, the Chakra whirred blindingly, as if spun by some core that burned with infinite heat. Along with them were many other gods whom Abhay did not recognize, at least three dozen arrayed up there, seated regally on heavenly thrones.

But amidst them was the one face that called out to Abhay the most- the scarred, battle-worn one of Parashuram, holding his Parashu that curved like a dark moon in that place of light, and yet amplified it. In his eyes was that same love that warmed Abhay's heart.

Then he felt it, as if the love had also words, had also plans, had also memories of the time they'd shared together.

I will meet you again, Abhay. I will meet you in your dreams, where I will visit. So will your mother.

In his hands, Parushram held the tablet.

It had been no dream, after all.

Then he saw Ira, standing a few feet away from him. She was looking up at the same scene, her mouth open in shock. As Abhay looked around, he saw all the other kids going about their normal activities, not paying any heed to the spectacular scene in the heavens that only Abhay and Ira could see.

Ira looked at him and their eyes locked.

Then she looked up and there was…a figure. It seemed like the blue of the sky collected with the whisps of the clouds, like illusory veils for the firmament, and together made a form that had the essence of the sky, and yet was like a phantom faintly silhouetted against it. But it was also something else- a creation of love that she felt spread through her heart, which was now awash with warmth as if the heavens had formed a blissful blanket over her unquiet mind.

It was her mother, Maya.

Vihaan was holding out a pack of chips towards Abhay, but Abhay ignored it and ran towards Ira. There was no need for words. Indeed, after what they had gone through together, it was hard to put all that was going through Abhay's mind into words. He hugged Ira tight and she hugged him back.

Vihaan dropped the pack of chips, aghast at the sudden change in his friend.

Abhay looked at Ira, smiling.

"You were willing to stay there and send me back."

She nodded.

"You were doing the same for me."

They looked up together at the scene in the sky and saw the gods looking down at them. Without realizing it, Abhay had held Ira's hand, and he felt her hand heat up, her fingertips glowing orange. Ira felt in her hand, not the soft hand of a schoolboy but the hardened grip of a mighty warrior. As the panorama in the sky began to fade, Abhay and Ira caught one last glimpse of Maya and Parushram. Then they looked at each other.

Their powers were intact!

As if reading their minds, Shiva's booming, majestic, melodious voice sounded in both their heads.

Be true to each other and use your powers wisely, for you may be called upon to serve again, guardians of the Kaalchakra.

AUTHOR'S NOTE

This did not begin as a book. It began with me asking myself a simple question.

How much do I really know about where I come from?

From a very young age, I've loved reading and have read about so many different cultures and peoples. Tales of the Iliad and Odyssey, of Beowulf and Gilgamesh, of Caesar and Genghis, fired my imagination, and stories of ancient Greece and Rome made me wonder about the amazing legacy those civilizations left behind.

Then, about two years ago, my parents gifted me a well-thumbed copy of *The Story of Indian Culture* by Bahadur Mal. Not just any book, but a book that was a signed copy gifted to my great-grandfather back in 1956. Sure, I'd read about Indian history in school and in books at home, but reading about the Vedas, about the rich legends and stories that were the foundation of our culture, made me wonder how much I really knew of our culture. That curiosity made me start reading more. I picked up translations of the *Ramayana* and *Mahabharata*, and then read even more, moving on to the *Shiva Purana* and others. The more I read, the more I was amazed at the richness of the stories and legends that made up our culture.

My generation is growing up in a world that is connected globally in ways past generations never experienced. Kids of my age cheer for the same sports stars no matter where they live, watch the same movies, spend time on the same social media apps, listen to the same music, and eat at the same fast-food chains.

However, does that mean we remain ignorant of, or even worse, apologetic about, our roots?

As I chatted with friends, I realized most of them were in the same boat I had been in. Vaguely aware of our legends and stories, but seeing them as relics of the past, with no connection to who we were and where we were headed.

In my book, *The Teen's Guide to Saving the World*, I explored the idea of how we as teenagers have a responsibility to create a better world- the world we will inherit as adults. The reading and exploration I did which led to this book taught me that our responsibility towards that future lies not just in how we can help create a fairer and more sustainable world, but also in the stories and values we will pass on to the next generation. One of the ways in which we can be in a position to do that is to appreciate and understand our own roots.

That's what *Kaalchakra* aims to do.

Of course, I hope this book entertains, but as with Abhay and Ira, I hope it makes all of us understand that we are not just defined by where we live now, the media we consume, the products we use and the jobs we do, but by that unbroken line that connects us to our ancestors, to our stories, to our roots.

I wrote this book with the motivation to share that with fellow teens, and I have many people to thank for the journey that has led to this book. First of all, my parents, for encouraging me to learn and question, and for always focusing on what really matters- the values we have and how we can use what we're passionate about to try and make a difference to others. I'd also like to thank Ms. Shweta Gupta, my English teacher in school, and my mentor, for her encouragement. Finally, a big thanks to Mr. Sagar Azad and the team at Anecdote Publishing, for their continued faith in me and for helping take this book to readers.

Aaditya Sengupta Dhar

November 2023

FURTHER READING

These are some of the books I read to learn more about our culture and roots. I hope some of you are inspired to pick a few of these up and join me in appreciating more fully the amazing heritage we have.

The Mahabharata. Translated by C. Rajagopalachari, Bharatiya Vidya Bhavan, 1958.

The Valmiki Ramayana. Translated by Bibek Debroy, Penguin Classics, 2018.

Shiva Purana. Translated by Bibek Debroy, Penguin Classics, 2023.

The Story of Indian Culture. Bahadur Mal, Vishveshvaranand Vedic Research Institute, 1956.

Mahagatha: 100 Tales from the Puranas. Satyarth Nayak, HarperCollins India, 2022.

Upanishads. Translated by Swami Paramananda, Prakash Publications, 2020.

The Essentials of Hinduism: An Introduction to all the Sacred Texts. Trilochan Sastry, Penguin Viking, 2022.

ABOUT THE AUTHOR

Aaditya Sengupta Dhar is a budding teenage author with five published books to his name and loves using his imagination to create fantastic new worlds. His first 'book' was a handwritten, stapled encyclopedia of ancient civilizations he wrote when he was eight, and seeing it displayed in the school library motivated him to keep writing and sharing his ideas. He wrote his first fantasy novel *Secret Tails (2018)* when he was ten years old. His next fantasy novel, *Legend of the Broken* Blade (2022), won critical acclaim, being selected as one of the 'Top 15 must-read books of 2023' by The Morning Standard, and was a bestseller.

Aaditya also aspires to use his writing to make a difference in causes he's passionate about. His 2020 eBook, *Underdogs*, raised awareness of the importance of helping underprivileged children unleash their potential, with all sales proceeds donated to Save The Children India. His 2021 book, *Back from the Brink*, was based on research funded by a micro-grant he won from MIT Solv[ED] and highlighted the largely unknown issue of animal extinction in urban areas and how we can all make a difference through simple, everyday steps. His 2023 book, *The Teen's Guide to Saving the World*, inspired teenagers to create a positive impact in their communities and won Silver at the Non-Fiction Book Awards in the US, besides being the #1 Bestseller in its genre on Amazon India.

Through *Kaalchakra*, Aaditya wants to make modern Indian youth feel that while we live in an increasingly globalized and interconnected world, we should always take pride in, and strength from, our cultural roots and heritage. A short story on this theme won a Gold Finalist Award at the prestigious Queen's Commonwealth Essay Competition in 2023.

When he's not writing books, Aaditya can be found working hard on his schoolwork, writing for the school magazine, following Cricket with a passion, and practicing Karate, in which he holds a black belt. Aaditya is fifteen years old and lives in Mumbai.